BLAKE KOURIK

ROACH

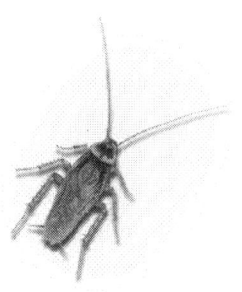

Copyright © 2025 by Blake Kourik

All rights reserved. No part of this publication may be reproduced, stored or transmitted in any form or by any means, electronic, mechanical, photocopying, recording, scanning, or otherwise without written permission from the publisher. It is illegal to copy this book, post it to a website, or distribute it by any other means without permission.

This novel is entirely a work of fiction. The names, characters and incidents portrayed in it are the work of the author's imagination. Any resemblance to actual persons, living or dead, events or localities is entirely coincidental.

First edition

"They're coming to get you, Barbara…"

- Night of the Living Dead (1968)

Acknowledgments

Many thanks to Makenna Goodman, Amanda East, Kendall Shelby, and Taylor Card for helping me bring this project to life.

1

He wanted a cigarette and that, above everything else, was what was sending him over the edge. It was 6:30 at night, he'd been on since 4:00 a.m., and he was damn tired. Damn tired. And now, slogging through this shit, all he wanted was a smoke, but he couldn't have one until he found this damn pipe. It'd been quiet in the office. Routine work. Rote. Muscle memory. Nothing out of the ordinary. Just the same shit, different day—boy, what a pun, you really are one clever schmuck, Rudy—until he'd gotten the call around 6:00 p.m. He'd been working pretty much alone at the facility, monitoring the equipment, functioning on autopilot, when his work phone rang, brrrrranging off in his pocket.

"Rudy. It's Jim. Got a problem that needs solved and you're it, buddy."

The call hadn't lasted long. Jim didn't have any more time on his hands than he did. The whole department was backlogged. It felt like they were constantly treading water just trying to keep their heads above the shit. It wasn't anything out of the ordinary, just a backed-up pipe, but since there simply wasn't enough manpower to allocate to the task, it was his and his alone. So, here he was, alone, in the sewer, at 6:30 in the evening, zipped up in Tyvek, wading through shit, trying to find where the hell he needed to be, and craving a goddamn cigarette more than anything.

The problem was the general public and the lack of education on the nation's sewers. That, and the fact that people just didn't care. They couldn't care, with the stuff they found down there. It didn't matter where you were, small town or metropolis, wherever the call was, you knew when you went down, you could be in for anything. Flushable wipes were the biggest culprits, because the companies advertised them as flushable, though they weren't. Beach whistles. Sewer balloons. Pads. Diapers, occasionally, and sometimes ever odder shit. Not all of it was always flushed. Sometimes the bigger things came in from the storm drains. But they all ended up at the same place. Down here in the dark. Clogging a pipe or blocking a drainage way. Causing problems.

Rudy'd heard stories. They all had. Stories about dead bodies, nasty things. He'd seen some, too. Things you didn't want to talk about. Things done in the bathroom, alone, flushed away. They were the ones to find them. Rudy had only seen one body in his time, in all twenty-seven years, but it'd been enough. It'd been on a routine job like this. Clogged pipe. He and a team had gone down and taken care of the issue. One of the main drains that connected to an apartment building had been backed up by a ball of flushable wipes. The ball had been about three feet in diameter, both horizontally and vertically across, and the fucker, sopping wet, soaked with piss and shit, had to have weighed five hundred pounds.

In the ball had been broken hypodermic needles, a few condoms, the regular stuff, but it'd been as they freed the wad of mess from the pipe that he saw what he'd heard so many stories about. A pale outline that slid out from behind the wad, into the muddy waters all around them. A small, thin snake of a body, almost translucent from soaking in the water so long, that slid from the pipe in the effluent. An aborted fetus.

No one else had seen it. As they pulled the wad free from the pipe, there'd only been a split second that anyone would've, as the freed fluids from behind the mess splurged into the sewage around them and flowed down the pipeline. But Rudy had. That'd been eight years ago.

Rudy aimed his torch down the stretching

pipeline and into the dark. The beam penetrated only so far. Behind him, the light from the streetlamps poured in through the open manhole cover. The pipe he needed was only supposed to be a few dozen yards ahead. It was a lateral, though to where, he couldn't guess. On the streets above, dozens of ancient apartment buildings lined both sides of the road, like looming monoliths. Directly above him was Delmar Street. He'd had to drive through the North side of town to get to the spot. Past Elm it was all rundown. Decrepit. Disused. Forgotten seemingly by the rest of the city. All except for the waste water department. Nothing was taken care of. Everything was simply rotting. Fallen away and neglected to time. Rudy guessed that the pipe ahead was just another casualty of dilapidation.

He pushed ahead, watching his step and in the far reach of his lantern, found the pipe he had set out for. A cast-iron lateral, jutting from the wall. Rust and slime caked the sides. Blackwater dripped steadily from the metal. To his left, waste water sat stagnant down the canal, reaching endlessly each way. Rudy adjusted his hardhat and stepped up to the pipe. It looked older than Jesus and as nasty as the devil. The brick that it protruded from sweat grease. Great black streaks ran down the wall from where it met with the pipe. Rudy held the flashlight up to the side and rubbed one gloved hand over the surface. A giant scab of metal fell away. He squatted and looked up. Under the pipe, a giant fissure ran along the bottom. In the middle, the pipe swelled. The metal contorted outward as if something had bent it out. It looked like a swollen bladder.

"What in the hell?" Rudy muttered.

He stood up and aimed his beam at the side of the pipe. Rudy inched forward. In the low light, he narrowed his eyes. His suit rustled about him. He leaned against the wall. In front of his shoes, the walkway that ran to both sides of the tunnel dropped off into water. The gray murk reflected the light from his beam, as did the slicked walls of the tunnel. Every surface sheened with sludge.

Rudy bit his lip and set his toolbox down. The pipe needed cut open to see what the hell was inside. He steadied himself, then bent down again, when a sharp pain pricked the side of his calf.

"Goddam—" he grit his teeth. A trickle of warmth ran down his leg. Something nicked him. Rudy twisted the lantern to see his leg. A black piece of metal stuck out of his skin. From the open tear, blood flowed out of his suit. A single tear of red streamed down the white nylon. Rudy bent down and pain flared up again from the gouge.

"Ow! Son of a bitch!"

Rudy set down the light. He sank against the wall and moved his leg into the beam. The metal in his leg twitched, then pulsated, and pain screamed up his leg again as it burrowed deeper. Rudy grabbed a hold of it and pulled. Between his fingers it squished. He yanked it free from his skin and blood streamed from the open wound. Thick, yellow sludge ran down his fingers as the thing gave way and crunched in his grip. Rudy held his hand in front of the light. Spined legs and bits of shell dripped from his fingers. Curds of intestines dropped to the floor.

Rudy's chest tightened. He drew his leg to the light. A dark black hole bore into his leg. From the wound blood seeped down into his shoe. A chunk was missing from him.

A bug...it was a goddamn bug....

Rudy pushed himself up. His heart hammered in his chest. A flake of metal clinked off his helmet. He turned his gaze. The pipe beside him swelled. More rust dusted off the corroded surface. The metal bulged and the fissure in the bottom widened. From the crack came a chittering noise. Something was pushing outwards.

Rudy aimed his beam at the pipe and watched as it burst. The crack erupted and black, oily water spewed from the bottom, down onto his feet. Droplets splashed onto the wall and climbed upward, clacking as they hit the brick and concrete. The wave surged up his legs, then crawled up his body. A million black legs pricked through his suit, before burrowing in.

The lantern dropped and rolled into sewage. Light lit up the murk of the canal as the lantern sank. Shadows played against the wall as Rudy became a writhing black mass.

Mouths chewed and bore into him. A million needles tore at his skin. His legs gave out beneath him. His mouth filled. His jaw opened to scream, but no sound came out. His lungs filled and the needles bore into his ears, his eyes, his chest. Everything turned to black and as the slow flowing sewage carried the lantern away, darkness settled in the tunnel again and silence filled the underground passage.

2

She was lost and that was the blunt truth of it. The unadorned reality. She hadn't the slightest idea where she was, or where she had been heading for the past two hours, and now she was somewhere downtown without any inkling as to where she might be, in a place she had never been before, all alone.

Yet despite all of this, Mary Joan didn't care. Ever since she got on the bus, her spirit had felt free. She felt a thousand times lighter. She felt young again, excited. She felt like she hadn't felt in a long time. She felt independent and that invigorated her. She felt like a woman of the world, making her own path.

For the past ten years, Mary Joan had been a resident of the Oak Shade retirement complex, and though she enjoyed it, she'd always felt restricted, though she never realized it. Not until she took this trip. Since she turned seventy-one, she'd been living at the complex. Once married, it'd been fifteen years since her husband died and they'd had no kids. George never had been able to give her a child, so when he passed, she'd been all alone. All their kin were either grown up or dead, and though relatives visited, no one ever offered to take her in. Not that they'd had to. She'd maintained her abilities. She went on walks every day, stayed engaged in the community, and kept her mind sharp. Mary Joan was a member of Oak Shade's cribbage club, president of the film committee, and co-chair of the neighborhood improvement association. In the summer, she swam every day, when she could, and in the winters she did yoga and Pilates indoors.

A busy body is an active body, and an active body is a healthy one, she always advised.

There was rarely a moment she wasn't doing something, and she liked it this way. It kept her going, physically and mentally. *Doing* was what made her happy. So, there wasn't a moment's hesitation when she learned of the opportunity to travel to Springdale to compete in their regional Boggle competition. Now although Mary Joan enjoyed all kinds of games—Yahtzee, Farkle, Skip-Bo, Uno, Phase 10, Cribbage—she was the reigning champ of Boggle at her complex. It was her favorite. *The Bogglin' Boggler*, her friends coined her, after she won the Elk's Club Tournament, two years ago, then the Senior's Tournament that South Windsor Expo held the year after. They weren't wrong either. That year, Mary Joan beat out all the competition and took home top prize—a three-foot-tall trophy that the complex displayed in their main lounge.

Mary Joan, 1st Place Champion, was engraved across the bottom, on a gold placard.

When she brought the trophy home, the complex's manager, Scarlett, had been the first to ask if they could place it in the lobby for everyone to see, to which Mary Joan had obliged.

"Our own local legend," Scarlett beamed after they had put it in the glass case alongside the complex's other memorabilia, "Mary Joan, the mind-bogglin' Boggler."

Her trip to downtown Springdale had been spur of the moment, and this added to her overall excitement. Not two days before, Scarlett had stopped her on her way back from swimming.

"Mary Joan. Come here, little girl," she wagged a finger at her like a co-conspirator.

In her hand, she'd held a flyer for the 10th Annual Open Invite Boggle Competition, to be held at the Springdale convention center on June 9th. Mary Joan had been toweling off her hair when Scarlett let her know that she'd already paid the admission cost.

"Called in today and signed you up. You're all set little girl. You go make us proud."

And just like that, she was in the competition. She packed her bags that night. The tournament was set to begin preliminary rounds Monday evening, with the second round on Tuesday, and the finals on Wednesday. Monday afternoon, she took an uber into town. Entry into the competition included room and board for three days at the Marriott Inn.

It took about an hour to get into town. During her ride, the driver asked where she was headed, then listened dutifully as she explained the occasion. She didn't say much to begin with, but once the driver—a young man from Ghana, named Jabez, whose smile lit up the cab each time he beamed—expressed genuine interest, it all flooded forth. She talked about her previous comps and when Jabez asked how well she did, she paused and grinned before stating that she had brought home the 1st place prize.

The trip into town breezed by as Jabez asked her about herself, and she asked him about his family. The two conversed and laughed and before she realized it, they were downtown Springdale. Jabez parked the car outside the front doors of the Marriott.

"Well, here we are, Ms. Joan," he said, "it was a

pleasure getting to know you."

Jabez wished her the very best of luck in her upcoming tournament, and when he helped her grab her bags from the trunk, she tipped him a twenty ("No, no, no, please Ms. Joan, this is far too much") and insisted that he keep it.

He thanked her again before parting ways. Then, Mary Joan carried her bags inside and checked into her room. It was only 1:00 p.m. when she changed clothes for the evening. The convention center was three miles away from her hotel. She decided she wanted to walk and with spring in her step, she headed out.

That was four hours ago. Now, close to day end—and surely, at the very least, 5:00 p.m.—with the first round of the tournament starting at 5:30 p.m., she had no idea if she was close to the convention center or not. Yet, she simply didn't care. It wasn't that she was blowing off the competition. She wanted to make everyone back home proud. There was just a certain part of her that felt liberated. As the warm summer breeze blew across the trees and through her hair, she closed her eyes. She felt really alive. Alive, like she hadn't, in quite some time. She felt lost and her wanderlust soared above the clouds in exhilaration.

Mary Joan opened her eyes. All around her, buildings towered. Above, birds swayed on roof edges and utility pole wires. The sun simmered low in the clouds. Cars shushed by on distant roads. In passing windows, she saw people working. Men and women at desks, typing at computers, taking phone calls. Her senses were filled. She took everything in and let her feet carry her nowhere, walking without a purpose, simply continuing forward. One foot after the other, she walked through downtown.

Before her, the city landscape yawned and stretched. The workday was coming to an end and the evening was beginning. Mary Joan thought back to when she was a child, living in Marshfield, growing up in a small town, a rural community that simply didn't exist as it once had in America. She remembered playing in the fields that her father owned, running through the rows of soybean and corn until her legs couldn't carry her anymore, and she collapsed to a heap on the ground and looked up to watch the clouds rolling above, sailing smoothly across the endless blue sky. She remembered the dizziness, the lightheadedness of staring up above her. She remembered running. That same feeling of jelly that came to her legs that she felt now. The same joyful tiredness. She remembered the breathlessness of her first kiss that came in those fields. Her first and only love. She thought of

George and her eyes welled, remembering his smile and the feel of his hand holding hers. He would've been proud of her. She knew he was proud of her.

Her eyes trailed up as she crossed the street and, on a whim, pivoted on the other side, taking a right. She followed the side of a glass building toward a giant tiered fountain. Up above, she knew her George was smiling down, waiting for her with open arms whenever the good lord decided to take her.

Mary Joan smiled. A fine mist sprayed her as she approached the fountain. She reached into her purse and dug around for her coin pouch. Her fingers toyed with the latch, before catching it, and poking inside. She took out a penny and closed the pouch again. In the water, she watched the waves ripple her reflection. She closed her eyes, wished, and tossed the coin in. Then, she carried forward.

Life was difficult, but beautiful, and every moment of joy was well worth the sorrow that led up to it. Nothing was meaningless, Mary Joan firmly believed. Everything had purpose. Everything happened for a reason. It had to. It just had to.

A tear dripped down her cheek and she absently wiped it away, lifting her gaze from staring at her feet, walking beneath her. Everything had purpose and God was good.

Mary Joan's eyes scanned the horizon, and amid the cluster of concrete and glass, signs, lights, wires, and fountains, they fell upon a large set of stairs. By the bottom stood a block of concrete, with an engraved metal sign: *Springdale Convention Center*.

A smile lit upon her expression again and widened.

There you are, Mary Joan. You let your feet do the walking, and they'll take you right where you need to go, she heard her husband, as clear as day.

It looked like she would be right on time to the first round of the competition after all, and she knew she would make everyone back home proud. Mary paused and glanced skyward once more. Above, the sun sank even further, bathing the skyline gold, tinging the clouds pink. It was beautiful. Simply beautiful.

Mary Joan walked forward toward the convention center. Mary Joan, the mind-bogglin' Boggler. A laugh escaped her. Her feet moved and her mind floated. Mary Joan, the mind-bogglin' Boggler. She laughed again, thinking of Scarlett, all her friends back home, and a seven-foot-tall trophy, with her name across the bottom. She giggled, imaging them all trying to fit it into a glass case that would never accommodate it. She chuckled and hoped she could bring it home to them. She hoped her wish would come true. Only time would tell.

    Mary Joan climbed the stairs to the convention center and with happiness in her heart, thinking of all her friends back home and the people who loved her, stepped into the building.

3

Music played from the small stereo in the corner of the kitchen as Lisa pulled dinner out of the oven and set it on the stovetop. Beyond the backyard, through the kitchen window, the sun dipped below the line of the trees bordering their property.

"Michael, it's about time for dinner," she called to her husband in the front office. He was at his computer, clacking away at the keyboard, finishing up some work for the evening while their son, Dylan, played outside with Kenneth, his best friend.

"Would you mind telling Dylan to come inside and wash up. We'll probably need to call Kenny's parents too, to let them know where he'll be if he wants to stay the night."

Lisa listened to the clacking in Michael's office continue, before calling again.

"Michael?"

"On it. On it," he answered, and the typing sped up, before stopping. Lisa listened to the office chair roll out then wheeze as Michael lifted himself up and walked to the front door.

She went to the island and pulled out the silverware drawer, grabbing another fork and knife for Kenny. She brought them both to the kitchen table and set them atop a napkin, right beside Dylan's place. A smile crossed her face. They were both good kids.

The salad sat in the center of the table. Forks, knives, and spoons were all laid out. Salt and pepper were out. Salad dressing. Butter. Rolls sat covered and ready in a wicker basket, beside the salad bowl. Tongs were ready.

"Oh!" Lisa said and went to the silverware drawer again. She took out a serving spatula for the meatloaf and brought it to the table. Then, she returned to the stovetop and grabbed the meatloaf, mashed potatoes, and two hot pads. She set them all on the table and placed her hands on her hips.

The front door opened, then closed.

"The boys ready, Michael?"

"I don't know. Didn't see them out there," he said and walked into the living room, headed straight for the phone.

"Do you think they went to Kenny's?"

"I don't know. That's what I'm about to find out. I'm sure they could've."

Lisa came close to Michael and wrapped her arms around his waist, listening as he dialed, the line rang, and Mrs. Kinnemann picked up.

"Laura? Hi, it's Michael. Say, did they boys come over to your place? They were just playing out front over here, but when I went out to call them in for dinner, I didn't find them."

No, they're not here, she heard Kenny's mother answer across the line, and she watched as the color fell from Michael's face and he said, "Okay. No. No, I'm sure they're out front still, then. We'll call back. Thank you."

Michael hung up the line and took to the front door with his wife. Lisa followed behind as he grabbed the flashlight from the office cabinet. He paced into the foyer, opened the door. She trailed him like a shadow and they both strode onto the brick steps of the porch, down onto the sidewalk, to the edge of the curb. The front door hung open behind them.

"Dylan?" Michael yelled.

"Dylan?" she yelled.

Nothing. Her husband stepped across the lawn. He ducked down into the bushes surrounding the electrical boxes to the house. He stood up.

"Dylan?"

Michael turned around and glared at the cul-de-sac. The streetlights blinked on, misting orange over the road. His eyes darted, wide, as round and as white as plates, from house to house.

"Dylan?!"

"Dylan?" she echoed, her eyes searching too.

Michael turned and strode back into the house. Lisa watched his silhouette through the windows grab his keys off the office desk. He pushed back out of the house, locked the front door behind him, and made for the car.

"Lisa, get in honey," he said, swinging into the vehicle. The engine came alive, and the headlights clicked on, bathing the driveway.

Lisa ran to the passenger's side. She threw herself in and Michael pulled out. He rolled the windows down.

"Dylan!" he yelled. Houses passed by, one after another. They blurred together as Michael drove on, and Lisa clung to her window.

"Dylan?!" she cried into the night.

Their tires spun, rolling over the quiet suburban streets. Doors began to open. Their neighbor, Brian Stevenson came out in his robe.

"Mike, Lisa, you two alright?"

Another door opened. Michael idled by the curb.

"We can't find Dylan," he said.

Brian nodded. "Let me get my keys," he said and ducked back into the house. When he came back out, his wife, Sara accompanied him.

"Everything all right?" a voice came from behind them. Another neighbor, John Hall, walked across his lawn.

"Dylan's missing," Brian said, and Lisa felt tears in her eyes well, then surge. They ran down her cheeks. Missing. Missing. Missing.

"Let me go grab Jane," he said and turned. "You two keep looking. We'll start calling everyone we can."

"You two go on," Brian said. "Sara called the police already. They're on their way. You keep looking around the neighborhood. Sara and I will search Paddock Oaks."

Michael nodded. Brian stepped away from the car and Lisa watched him and Sara duck in their own. Michael pulled away from the curb. In the low light, Lisa saw the tears streaming down his own face. He leaned out the window again.

"Dylan?!"

The streets flowed by, and night fell like a curtain. Darkness crowded the houses. Shadows stretched in their headlights.

Her baby was missing. Dylan was missing. She leaned out the window and called to her baby with her husband, but her lips were numb. Her mouth moved and her voice called. Her throat scraped with each yell, calling to her child as night fell and the moon rose, but she felt none of it. Her mind raced. Her baby was missing, and the roads passed by and on none of them were her child. They passed beneath the oak trees, lining the sides of the streets. Her eyes searched and as they finished checking their neighborhood, coming to the start of their circle drive again, getting out of the car, and meeting John and Jane at the front of their house, now accompanied by two policemen, and Kenny's parents, she sobbed, as her husband told the police the last time that they had seen Dylan, and that no, he wasn't anywhere he normally would be, and everything fell from her grasp. She collapsed inward and as her husband spoke to the police, she thought of her baby's face. His smile. His eyes.

Her baby was gone. Her baby was gone and she didn't know where he was and her thoughts reeled and everything faded from her. Dylan.

My baby's gone. My baby's gone.

And everything that could have happened, did, in her mind. Everything that could have happened to her baby played across her eyes, and she sobbed, and her husband grabbed her as she fell and everything faded, and her world went to black.

4

He had never been there before and couldn't remember exactly how they had gotten there, but he knew they would find their way back. No matter how far they ventured, they always found their way back before dark, and the sun was still high enough in the sky that Dylan knew they'd be able to make it home in time before the streetlights came on.

But they'd never ventured this far. Normally, they kept to their neighborhoods. Either near his house or Kenny's. This was neither one, however. They'd started halfway between their houses, playing Cops and Robbers, running down the streets. Neither one of them had any specific plan in mind. They tucked down avenues, ducked behind bushes, hid behind trees, and laughed the whole way. Then, somewhere along their journey, Kenny looked at Dylan, laughed and bolted down a side street, and Dylan had followed him, running after his friend, until the two exhausted themselves, and they fell back to a walk, panting and sweating.

The houses around them changed in size and shape. Lawns too, and the street beneath them. As they continued walking, the houses shrunk from two story Victorians to squat, one story domiciles, neglected and angry looking. Upright, wooden fences turned to chain-link barriers and warped boards. Green lawns grew yellow and balding. Porches accumulated trash and couches and bikes. Cars rusted, parked cattywampus in dirt front yards, pulled right up to the houses. Broken windows and boarded up doors marred every home.

Kenny pushed ahead, walking down the street. Dylan dragged behind him. His legs hurt. In his shoes, his feet ached from running so far. He was exhausted.

Kenny's head tilted upward, watching the clouds. As he reached the end of the street, he stopped and looked back. A smile grew on his face, squinting his eyes.

"I think we need to go back," Dylan said.

Kenny looked him over and his smile widened. "Catch me if you can!" he said and bolted, turning down the intersecting street.

"Kenny! Wait!" Dylan said and ran after him. His converse slapped against the pavement, kicking up loose gravel. Kenny's laughter echoed down the avenue. At the stop sign, Dylan looked both ways for cars, but saw none.

No vehicles came or went on the street that they were on. Only a low hum of engines, from farther away, rippled the air. Not even any birds sung. Quiet sat like a thick gel in the air.

Dylan turned the corner and ran after his friend, far down the adjoining street already, growing smaller in the distance. His breath heaved in and out of his lungs. Both of his legs felt like they were on fire. His heart hammered. Sweat poured down his face.

"Kenny!"

The road twisted and Kenny disappeared from his view. Dylan sprinted after him. As he rounded the corner, he saw Kenny stopped in the center of the road. He looked down at the street.

"Kenny! We need to go back!"

Kenny looked up at him, then back down at the asphalt. The same grin doubled on his face. He turned around and dropped to his hands and knees. Dylan watched as his friend sank into the street. His legs disappeared, then his torso, then his shoulders. Kenny turned and looked at him as his head sank beneath the road. His laughter echoed.

Dylan ran toward the hole. A white van was parked by it on the side of the road. His feet flew beneath him. As he reached the hole, he looked through the window of the van inside. No one was in it. Atop the asphalt, a metal cover that someone had pried up, laid by the side of the hole. It was a sewer entrance. Someone was down there. Whoever drove the van was down in the hole. Dylan looked down into the darkness but saw nothing.

"Kenny!" he called. Silence answered him. He dropped to his stomach atop the street and lowered his head to the lip of the manhole. "Kenny?"

A whimper came from the dark. "Dylan?" issued forth, barely a whisper. "Dylan?"

"Kenny, get out of there!" he whispered back.

"Dylan…please…"

Ice ran down Dylan's spine. His arms and legs stood out in goosebumps. Every hair on his body raised. Sweat slicked his shirt to his skin like cellophane. His mouth went dry.

"Kenny?" he whispered. His voice echoed down the manhole. From the concrete walls of the underground entrance, metal rungs protruded. Dylan gazed down into the darkness.

He swallowed and his throat scraped. Another whimper issued from the depths. Dylan swung his legs over the opening in the street and stepped onto the first rung. His feet moved beneath him, descending the ladder. One foot after another, he climbed down. His hands gripped the slick metal rungs. His foot slipped and he caught himself under his arm. The metal rung scraped his side, grinding against his ribs. Bright, hot pain flared up under his arm. Air wheezed in and out of his lungs, pushing through clenched teeth. His eyes slammed shut. Tears dripped from his eyes. He began to cry.

Dylan placed one foot down on the next rung, then the other, then again, until he reached the bottom. His shoes touched concrete, and he let go of the ladder.

"Kenny?" he said, and his voice came out as a sob.

The sound of running water trickled before him. As his eyes adjusted to the darkness, shapes and outlines grew from shadow. Under his feet, a narrow walkway extended left and right, as far as he could see. At the toes of his shoes, the walkway ended and dropped off into a ravine of running water, too thick and dark to see the bottom. On the other side of the river ran another walkway, impossible to reach, without falling in the murk. Dylan didn't know how deep the ravine ran. He couldn't see the bottom. His eyes turned upward.

Above his head, the manhole formed a dot of fading light in the surrounding darkness. The sun was setting. Through the opening, Dylan watched color fade from the sky. He pushed himself up against the wall of the tunnel. Beneath his hands, the wall squirmed with moisture. A thick slime coated the brick. It soaked into his shirt and his pants, hot and wet. Dylan's breath shuddered from his chest.

A thick stench hung in the air. With every breath, he heaved the odor in. The humid air filled his lungs, gagging him. His throat clenched and his gorge surged. He felt like he was going to vomit. His fingers sunk into the muck covering the wall.

"Kenny…" he choked.

He clenched his eyes shut.

"Dylan…" whispered the dark.

Dylan opened his eyes. On a volition of its own, his head turned toward the sound. Down the walkway, further, he saw a figure on the ground, crouched over, huddled in a ball.

"Kenny?"

The figure shivered.

"Kenny?"

Dylan crept along the walkway. He pressed his back against the wall of the tunnel, his eyes glued to the flowing water in front of his feet. One slip and he would go in. Then, down, down, down. Down below the murk. Drowned. Dead. He watched the running water, then pulled his eyes back toward Kenny. His friend's body was pressed up against the wall, tucked inward. Both of his arms wrapped around his knees. His chin tucked into his chest. His back faced Dylan.

Dylan edged further down the walkway, sideshuffling his feet. One step at a time. Kenny didn't move. He looked behind himself as he got closer to Kenny and farther and farther away from the ladder. The light from the manhole dampened to almost nonexistence. A soft orange glow sept in from above. The streetlights had come on. They were supposed to be home by now.

Dylan reached Kenny and lowered himself against the wall. He squatted to his knees, his butt against the brick.

"Kenny?" he placed a hand on his friend's shoulder.

Kenny turned toward Dylan. Tears streamed down his face. Wide eyes glared from his sockets. His lip quivered. "Dylan…" he said. He turned and looked down the tunnel and Dylan's eyes followed.

Before them, on the thin strip of walkway, a tattered, white suit stretched across the concrete. From the sleeves of the suit, two arms protruded. Bone white, skeletal hands extended. Fingers reached out, curled at the tips. Dylan could see scratch marks in the grime on the ground. Jagged lines where the fingers had clawed. His eyes traced the arms of the suit to the shredded collar. A skull jutted from the neck. Its jaw hung open. It had died screaming. It died crawling away from something, mouth open, screaming.

Kenny whimpered.

"Kenny, we need to go…" Dylan said. The words pulled from his mouth, as if by string. His lips moved without his control. "Kenny…"

He pulled at his friend and Kenny sobbed. "Dylan…" he said and pointed at the body.

A high-pitched chittering arose in the dark. The suit covering the body rustled. The back distended, then lowered again, breathing. Kenny pushed himself back on his hands and butt. From the arm of the suit, a small, black jewel emerged and scuttled down the length of the hand. It stopped at the fingers and twisted up on its hind legs. Its antennae twitched. Its palps vibrated.

It ran down the bones onto the concrete and crawled up Kenny's shoe.

"Dylan! Get it off me!" he yelled and scrambled backward. He slapped his legs as the bug circled up his jeans. "Get it off!"

Kenny stood. He smacked at his torso as the bug twisted up. It ran over his jacket, toward his face. "Dylan!" he screamed as it reached his neck. He stumbled backward and his foot slipped. His legs went out beneath him. His shoulder hit the concrete and he rolled into the murk.

"Kenny!" Dylan screamed.

His body sunk beneath the surface. Dylan could see nothing. The running water, a thick oil, black glass, threw his rippled reflection back at him. A hand shot out from the murk. Dylan leaned over the edge and grabbed it. Kenny's head rose above the surface. His other arm shot out of the sewage. Dylan grabbed his palms.

Slick grease squelched between their hands. Kenny's grip loosened and he slipped into the water again. His body bobbed down.

"Dylan!"

The words were choked off by the water.

Kenny's hands shot out of the river. Fingers gripped the edge of the walkway and his body rose up out of the effluent. His mouth hung open, his head slicked over with sludge. Beads of oil clung to him like sequins. A million, scintillating scales covered his skull, moving, pulsing. The inside of his mouth squirmed, alive. Dylan could see no skin. Only the writhing scales. One of the scales detached from Kenny's skull and skittered onto the walkway. His body sunk again.

Dylan scattered backward as Kenny sank beneath the murk. His body disappeared beneath the current and the detached sequin scurried toward him, twitching, chittering. He pushed himself to his feet and ran toward the ladder. From the edge of the walkway, where Kenny's body had sunk, a black wave rose out of the water and flowed toward his feet. The chittering echoed in the tunnel to a deafening screech.

Dylan lunged for the bottom rung. The shining wave pulsed over the concrete. His hands gripped the metal. He pulled himself up. Beneath him, the mass surged against the wall and climbed upward. The horrible chattering rang in his ears, an unending, unearthly tone. Ghastly odors filled his nostrils. Sewage. Waste. Sick, sweet decay. The odor of rotting fruit, tinged with chemicals. Dylan choked. Rung after rung, he pulled himself up and his arms screamed. His legs burned. Every muscle felt on fire. His throat swelled to a pinhole. He gagged as the living tide flowed up his feet.

Legs pricked up him. Endless spines dug through his clothes, into his skin. Warmth sept down his legs as he climbed to the surface. His feet gained weight as the swarm swallowed his shoes. Layers of scales covered his ankles. Dylan pulled himself up the ladder toward the street. Dull orange light hit his eyes. Fresh air filled his lungs. He grabbed the lip of the manhole.

His fingernails dug into the asphalt and broke off from their beds. He pulled himself out onto the street and the mass surged up his legs. Under his jeans, they crawled up him, higher. Inside his shoes, lightening pain flared. His body screamed. A million drills bore into him. A million razors lacerated him, again and again. His vision swam. Circles of gray filled his sight. His eyes rolled up into his head. His ears filled with the endless, inhuman screech. Pain gored into his ears as his eyes blinked out.

I want my mommy. I want my daddy...

He dragged himself across the road, until his arms gave out. His legs stopped moving. He couldn't feel anything. He couldn't feel his body. All sound faded away. His vision stopped.

Mommy, daddy...I want to go home...I want to go home...

And all thoughts stopped.

5

If I could just have a drink...

The bottle had run out hours ago and the tremors had already begun. His hands went first. On the handle of his shopping cart, they'd started to shake as he pushed his belongings along the road. Every crack in the pavement sidewalk, every cleft that caused the cart to bump, sent horrible vibrations up his arms. Then, every footstep had started to hurt. He needed a drink. About a mile down the road, he'd given up his cart and left it on McDaniel Street, tucked into an alley, covered in cardboard. Nobody would take any of his things. Now, he shambled along the road.

His matted hair clung to his shoulders. Sweat dripped down his face, through his beard. His clothes slicked to his skin and his eyes hurt. Too dry. Too dry. He needed a drink. God, he just needed a drink. His mind had given up. He had no change. No money on him. Nothing to help. Mercy was a whisky bottle. Wild Turkey.

Warm liquid that lit the throat on fire and eased the wind and made the body stop. The spirit was willing, but the body was weak, and that was what Father Matheson had preached to them all so many Sundays ago, but now his body was dead, his spirit was willing, but his body was gone. So many Sundays ago, he had been just a child. Just a boy, attending mass with his parents. Back when everyone was still alive. Back before the accident. Back before he'd lost his job. His house. His life. Everything.

Theo, look out!

He'd been on the line, working the chains, when the pulley broke and the pipe fell. Five years of his life. A broken spine. Crushed clavicle. Pulverized ribcage. Theodore Culbert fell off the wall. Theo Culbert had a great fall. And all the doctors said he was lucky to be alive and that it would take time, time to heal again. That he should consider himself lucky, thank God, and praise him for the miracle he brought: his life.

Five years went into learning to walk again, and the company paid for all medical expenses, but when he went into physical therapy, the money dried up. Insurance took care of what it needed to, then the company withdrew. For six months, he sat immobile in a hospital bed, unable to do a thing for himself. A vegetable. Then, the nurses came in and his arms and legs were moved for him, and drugs were intravenously fed into him, but nothing took away the screaming, horrible pain of stretching muscles that had remained immobile for months, moving what had laid inactive for days, weeks, months again.

Laying there, every day, he wanted to die. All while everybody told him how lucky he was. All while tears streamed down his face. All while his bill racked up and up and up.

And then they made him stand again, and he did, and the worst pain he'd ever known was inflicted upon him daily, learning to move again on his own. He could do nothing. Only a few footsteps, starting off, before it became unbearable. And every day, it was a few footsteps more. A few footsteps more. A few footsteps more, before he could move around comfortably for five minutes or more. Then ten minutes. Then, half an hour. Then, without someone supporting him.

The walker came, then the cane, then finally, his own two legs. But the pain never left him. Theo gritted his teeth and pushed through it all.

The lord smiled down upon you, Theo.

But it wasn't God that had helped him. It was himself. It was him who learned to walk again. And God never took the pain away. Even when he left physical therapy, and the nurses and doctors were all so proud, and he was their miracle case, the pain never left. He told them, but it never affected their outlook. He was God's miracle.

So, they sent him home with a prescription, and when he insisted that the pain remained, they told him that—

It takes time, Theo, it takes time...

—so, he dealt with the pain the only way he could, by medicating with the only thing that helped.

Eventually, what once numbed the constant, sharp, grinding pain in his back, grew useless. Over time, it took more and more to dampen the agony of every movement.

Everything fell from him. First his car went, then his house to pay for the bills. He watched himself lose it all but couldn't keep sober enough to go back to work. The pain never left without alcohol, and even the alcohol barely helped. Pain was a constant unless he'd drunk enough to not feel anything. Everything fell from his grasp and as he fell to the streets, he found he couldn't care. There was nothing left of him to care. He'd given everything, but the pain never left. He was God's miracle, but he wished he were dead. If the pipe would've killed him when it fell, it would've been a blessing. But God had no mercy.

Theo's lids flickered over his eyes. His hands hung by his sides as he staggered forward. His vision warbled. His tongue stuck to the roof his mouth. He felt himself going.

Up ahead, on the street before him, a white van was pulled off by the side of the road.

There could be a bottle inside... something spoke from beyond him, himself, but not his own.

There could be. There could be.

He pushed himself forward and his spine screamed. Every finger trembled. Beneath his body, his legs felt weak, giving. Everything shook. Under his shoes, he felt every piece of loose gravel shift. His feet hurt and he was dry. So, dry. His finger and toenails felt as if they were prying themselves loose from their nailbeds. Each tooth in his mouth ached. Throbbed.

The van grew steadily closer. The streetlights had already come on. There was no one in sight. All around him, the streets were silent. Abandoned buildings and forgotten houses lined both sides of the avenue. Weeds grew in dead front lawns and the street alike. Everything was broken. In the surroundings, the van stood out, pristine.

None of its windows were broken. All four tires, still intact. None of the rims were missing. It didn't sit up on cinderblocks. No rust ate through the hull. It looked running. New.

Theo circled around to the passenger's side window and peered in the glass. He squinted. The van was empty. Equipment lined the walls of the rear cab. No one was inside, though. He tried the door handle. It gave and the door clicked open.

Theo pulled it toward him and ducked inside. He climbed into the passenger's seat. Out of habit, he pulled down the driver's sun visor. A pair of keys fell down into the seat. He peered behind himself. Tools and appliances filled the back of the van. He tried the glovebox. Locked. His fingers fumbled with the keys, then inserted them into the lock. He twisted. The door fell open and the light came on. Inside the compartment, among papers and a gun was a small glass bottle. A half pint of Jack.

Theo grabbed the bottle and twisted off the lid. It fell to the floorboards. He brought the bottle to his lips and threw his head back. Whiskey poured down his throat. His mouth filled with fire. His insides warmed. Smooth, sweet, burning honey coated his gullet. The shaking in his hands faded to minor vibrations. The pain in his back grew further from him, a sinking sun on distant horizon. Pervading warmth became all he could feel. Just the warmth of whiskey. Mercy. Forgiveness.

Theo drained the bottle and let his hand holding it fall to his side. His head fell back against the headrest. His fingers relaxed. The bottle fell from his grasp. It bounced out of the van and skid across the asphalt. His eyes closed. Just the warmth remained. All feeling felt far from him. Loose at the controls. Relaxed. Free from the grip of pain.

His head filled with the static of his own ears. Nothing moved. Nothing sounded. All was quiet. Silent, slow, peaceful ships sailing on the horizon. Theo drifted and lace gauze wrapped him, soothing his nerves. Only warmth gripped him. Warmth carried him.

A thin static buzzing filled his ears, tinging the night.

Cicadas...

Theo thought of being a child, at his grandparent's house. Spending days in the summer, out at their home. Being away from the city. Sleeping with the windows opened. And the sound of cicadas. Cicadas ringing. A constant noise that scored each night. But this wasn't the same sound.

The static continued. A constant hissing, not like electricity, not a constant humming, but a steady chittering, as of mouths chewing. A low screeching. Like metal on metal. Brakes scraping. Sparks sending up.

Not cicadas.

Theo opened his eyes and turned his head toward the sound.

Outside the van.

His head lolled to the left. His eyes slid down the window. The sound was coming from outside the driver's side door. He pushed himself out of the passenger's side seat. His body felt heavy and dumb. His feet hit the pavement and he stumbled forward, falling into the weeds that lined the sidewalk. A thick mat of growth covered the pavement. The sound was louder now, closer to the ground. Fiercer. Theo rolled onto his back. The sky was dark now. Light pollution tainted the black of the night. Thin whisps of clouds scattered above.

He looked to his right, under the van, and in the middle of the road saw a hole in the ground. An open manhole. The cover sat beside it. Beside the opening laid a mass on the ground. A pile of clothes. A small body.

Theo's eyes widened and he sat up. It looked like a child. A child on the ground. He staggered to a stand and hit the side of the van. The warmth remained, but his mind was alive. He circled around the front of the vehicle. In front of the van, the body laid facedown. It looked like a small boy.

Theo squinted. In the dark, he could just make out the shoes. Red, tattered converse. Jeans covered the legs. A long sleeve yellow t-shirt clung to the body. Flowing brown hair fell to the shoulders. Theo's lip quivered. He squatted down.

The hissing was louder, now. The low buzz. It

was louder but muffled, coming from under the body.

His throat tightened. His hand reached out. The chittering sept from the body. He grabbed the boy's shirtsleeve and pulled.

The body rolled over with a sickening ease. One limb toppled over and smacked the concrete. Dead weight flipped. The boy's head cracked against the asphalt. Theo looked into the boy's eyes. Both were clouded over. The jaw fell open and the hissing grew louder.

The boy moaned. Air slipped from the throat. The chest vibrated. Under the clothes, the stomach distended. The face bulged outward, as if filling with water. Skin stretched. The mouth opened wider. Both eyes rolled backward into the head. The shoulders arched, and the body screeched, a thin ripping sound, like peeling Velcro. The throat puffed outward, and the horrible chittering rose to an inhuman squeal.

Theo stumbled backward and the shirtsleeve ripped off in his hand. The body collapsed and melted to oil. The boy's face disappeared. The stomach popped and black liquid flowed from the clothes, covering them. Shining droplets spewed from the sleeves and spread over the asphalt. White skin disintegrated to bones. The dark wave flowed over his feet.

On further roads, cars zoomed by, and motorcycles roared, ripping down main stretches. Empty streets extended and under the traffic, no one heard the screams in the night.

6

Time drug by like a knife, bleeding him slowly. His eyes flicked through the glass wall of his office to the sales floor downstairs. On ground level, five associates wandered around, helping customers, tidying up exhibits, fixing what needed to be fixed. Wasting time, ultimately, just like he was. Filling the minutes, hours, and days, peddling bullshit. Selling furniture to the ever-hungry clientele. For the past hour, he'd done nothing, really, except return a few calls to potential wholesalers and clients that were interested in commercial offers. Bigger fish, his boss would say.

"You know how to reel 'em in, Matt, so reel 'em in, boy," Mr. Ordner always laughed and clapped him on the back, his spotless polo shirt tucked in over his hanging gut.

Matthew shoved the portfolio from Central containing all the outlines on numbers, sales, commissions, and how well their branch was doing in the top drawer of his desk. He picked up his coffee mug, sipped, then grimaced and set it back down. Cold. He didn't want any coffee anyways. It wouldn't help.

He didn't have any motivation left in him to get anything done for the rest of that day. There were several people he still needed to call, several looming tasks that he could chip away at, always things to do, but he didn't want to, and the truth was, none of them were pressing. They could all wait until tomorrow. His motivation always died toward the end of the day. Come in at 9:00 a.m., hump it until 3:00 p.m., then half an hour for lunch. Clock back in at 3:30 p.m. Then, at 4:00 p.m., regardless of coffee, motivation ran out, along with energy. Usually, he would drink another cup to get him through, and often it helped, but on some days it didn't and today just happened to be one of those days.

So, he watched, keeping his body positioned facing his computer screen and his desk, so he could turn his head if anyone looked up. He skimmed through his feed, keeping an eye on his email, watching the time, watching customers amble around the showroom floor, and hoping that every call that rang through was one for the sales floor, one that could be taken care of by an associate downstairs, so he wouldn't have to answer it. Not that it was beyond him, as supervisor, to answer sales calls and fill in where needed. It was his job to lead the team. Be a team player. Take the reins.

This afternoon, however, he didn't want to. The bottom right corner of his desktop read 6:37 p.m. The last hour always dragged by the slowest. He wondered how many Americans did the exact same thing at their own jobs. How many skated by, trying to make it through another day, without being too exhausted when they got home to do anything else. He cared and he didn't care. It didn't matter. It was all bullshit. Not all of it, but most of it. Same shit, different day. He enjoyed helping the clients. Getting to know their names, helping make things work, snagging new accounts. He enjoyed making the sale and selling people a good piece of furniture, or a set, or furnishing an office place with quality equipment. It felt good to make ensuring that the clients were getting quality furnishings, rather than the shipped junk from overseas, but it still wore on him some days–ealing with the public–because for every easy client, for every customer who was kind, thankful, and a pleasure to work with, there were fifteen more who weren't. There were uptight wives, disgruntled clients, walk-ins off the street who had no interest in buying anything at all, and people who wanted you to understand that your prices were shit and that they wouldn't buy from you if you were the last storefront on earth. Assholes in short. Assholes everywhere. It didn't matter where you were.

Matthew fiddled with a pen. His thumb slid under the clip and flicked upward. The clip snapped against the metal cap. He set the pen down and looked toward the sofa section of their downstairs department. By the loveseats, a heavyset woman, waddled over to one of their new-hires and planted her hands on her hips. He couldn't hear what she said, but her expression said enough. The woman's eyes became slits and her mouth puckered. Red rose in her cheeks. Animation gripped her face. She pointed to the sofa behind her and gave the new-hire a look. The kid's name was Clayton. Clayton stammered something, smiled apologetically, then turned and darted to grab their sales floor manager, Brandon.

Matthew sighed and twisted around back at his desk. He simply wasn't there. It'd been growing harder for him recently at his job because he was tired of pushing ahead, bulldozing through, and getting it done whether he liked it or not. For most of his adult life, that was how he'd operated. His mantra, for as long as he could remember, had been: *Just get the job done. Put your head down, get your shit done, and do your best. Don't complain. It doesn't matter if you like it or not.*

But more and more recently, he couldn't fake it. He couldn't bulldoze through like he used to. The motivation to do more simply didn't exist. It all faded. He did what was required, but nothing more, and more and more recently, he felt himself burning time, watching the clock, waiting for the bell.

He swiveled in his chair and grabbed a tissue. His right nostril dripped, running down his lip and he caught it with a tissue. His allergies had been acting up recently too, and the underside of his nose was red from wiping it all day long. Another grain of sand in his sandwich. Another drop in the bucket, but they added up.

He didn't know what he was going to do, but he felt that something, somewhere, soon, was going to give. Had to give. He would never do enough of nothing to get fired– he couldn't bring himself to do that– so that left two options: either he would find another gig elsewhere, or he would stay where he was, biding his time and sitting on his thumb. Doing nothing until 7:00 p.m. day after day.

Matthew crumpled the tissue and threw it in the trash. He logged off his online session, shut off the computer, and checked his phone.

6:52 p.m.

Close enough. He pushed in his chair and walked

toward the stairwell. As he trailed toward the upstairs door, Jody, their inventory accountant, leaned over to look through his door.

"See you tomorrow, Matt," he said and waved through the door frame. Matthew waved back and paced down the stairs. His dress shoes treaded over the green carpet. He pushed out the side door and into the parking lot. Bright sunlight, dying on the horizon, blinded him, and he squinted and looked both ways. No cars came his way. In the front parking to his left, a burly man climbed out of a Ford F-150. Across the street, cars pulled into the McDonald's, circling around the building, waiting in line.

Matthew stepped out and zipped toward his car. He pulled his keys out of his pocket. His thumb hit the fob. The doors unlocked. He dropped inside, closed the door beside him and stared ahead. The cab was like an oven. Bumps raised on his skin as he sat in the heat that the sun had radiated into the cab all day. It felt good after sitting in the cold air conditioning. He closed his eyes and leaned back against the headrest.

Something had to give.

Matthew turned his keys in the ignition and rolled down the window. A slight breeze ruffled the air. It felt beautiful out. For the past few weeks, it felt beautiful out and every day he sat inside. In the vacant lot that abutted their loading dock, a young man on a bicycle stood and pumped his pedals, bumping over the grass. Powerlines buzzed above. At the Fazzoli's, near the exit to the highway, an employee lugged a bulging black garbage bag to the dumpster. Matthew watched the kid drag the bag, struggle with the lid, then with hefting the load into the dump. The kid heaved the bag up with his shoulder, used his free arm to lift the lid, and succeeded with tossing the bag in, before falling on his ass. Matthew smiled when he saw the kid laughing. He had a good sense of humor at least. Matthew envied him.

He listened to the traffic on 60. Noise from the highway drowned out almost all other sounds. Brakes that needed replaced screeched on the main drag. A few horns honked. Lots of cars with souped-up exhaust pipes ripped by, loathsomely.

He didn't want to go home. He put the car in reverse and backed out of his space. His hand shifted the gear to drive. He pulled out of the lot. There wasn't anywhere in particular he wanted to go. Just not home. He felt like driving for a while and not thinking.

Matthew took a left out of the parking lot and turned onto E Independence, rather than pulling out onto S Weller. The radio played at a low volume, and he twisted the knob, cranking the music. Soft rock flowed from the speakers. He opened the sunroof, grabbed his shades from their compartment, and threw them on. At the light, he continued forward, and the road stretched on before him.

Sun shone through his windows, lapping at the car. Few clouds crowded the blue sky. It was warm out. Not hot, but wonderfully warm. Matthew sunk back in his car seat and rode, resting his foot on the gas, cruising down the boulevard. He let his mind drift, and at the turn he normally took to go home, he kept going straight, following the drag.

The breeze whipped his hair and music carried his thoughts. He thought of nothing. He only drove. The road carried him, a pinpoint on the horizon, a never-ending path. With no destination in mind, he watched it unfold. He let his mind melt into the black of the asphalt, the feel of the engine through his foot on the pedal, and the warmth of the sun, setting, on his skin and he coasted on.

7

Good. Great. Grand. Wonderful. That was just what he needed this afternoon. Exactly what he wanted. Another problem. More shit to deal with.

Liston glared across the room at the floor drain where the first one sat looking at him. Right before the toe of his non-slip shoe, the second one froze, a splotch on the tile. Sick, shining translucent brown against yellowed, chipped white. He lunged forward and slammed his foot down, squashing the insect. It crunched under his sole.

He looked across the room at the second bug. It didn't move, only stared up at him, unafraid. Then, in the silence of the back kitchen, he heard it hiss. The goddamn thing hissed clear as day. Like a feral cat it stood on its hind legs, rising like a cobra, and hissed a hitch pitched squeal.

Liston lunged forward to squish it and the bug skittered down the drain. He looked back toward the entry to the kitchen, where he squashed the first. Gunk trailed in the tread of his shoe from where he killed it to where he stood. On the floor, thick, chunky curd and smashed brown shell sept in the grout. He lifted his shoe to inspect the damage. The crevices of his sole were lined with the muck. The fuckin thing was full of guts that exploded when he squished it. His nose wrinkled. It smelt godawful. A frothy aroma like spoiled milk, boiled broccoli, rose up to his nostrils.

He set his foot back down and took off his shoe. His eyes traced across the kitchen. Under the sink was a container of Clorox wipes. He walked across the room, feeling the cold tile through his sock, grabbed three wipes, and went to work on the guts. God, the stuff stunk.

He wiped up where he'd squashed the bug, then went to work on the trail he left. After cleaning the first spot, he went back for more wipes. Cleaning the initial splat took up all three. He scooped the bug's insides up with the wipe, tossed them in the trash, rinsed, repeated, then came back with two more wipes to clean up the residue. It took five wipes total. Five wipes.

Liston glared at the other three steps he took and the gunk on the floor that he'd tracked across the kitchen.

Just great, he thought as he wiped up the other spots, *and the other one got away.*

That meant there were more of them, since

there'd been two. Where there was one, there were more. And there'd been two. Great. Just great.

*Go tell your friends, fucker...*he stared at the drain.

Liston threw away the wipes and surveyed the kitchen. The floor looked better. He picked up his shoe. It would have to be rinsed off, but not in here. Not in the kitchen. Outside with a hose. He had a second pair of shoes in the trunk of his car. These would have to go in a plastic bag until he could get home and clean them.

His other shoe came off and he went to the closet. A box of black garbage bags sat eye-level on the shelf. He pulled one from the roll and whipped it open.

He'd have to call an exterminator immediately. There was no way in hell anybody was going to find out. No employees, nothing. He'd schedule a time for them to come out, get the place hosed down, sprayed, and the fuckers exterminated.

Maybe it was a fluke. They'd both come out of the drain, so maybe there weren't any in the actual building, but the rock in his gut told him it could be otherwise, and it burnt him up inside. There was always something. Always something, always some shit that he had to deal with. Something that got in the way, put him back. It felt like every step he took forward he was pushed two steps backward.

For seventeen years, he'd poured his sweat, blood, and tears into the joint, and every inch of the way, there'd been someone or something trying to stop him. Stumbling blocks that wanted him to fail. Competition at every corner.

But nothing ever brought him down. Not the dozens of other Chinese joints that opened along the same street as his, slinging the same product, offering the same food—but shit quality, street meat, cat-chew-chicken. Not the constant construction that the city pulled. Not the access ways to his business that were shut down for months on end. Not even fucking COVID. He'd survived all of it. All the shit. Every hangup. He'd been there since the beginning, and he'd ridden it all. He was a local. Not a goddamn tourist, along for the ride. He was the real deal, but on days like this, he wondered if it was worth it.

No one was there except for him. No one knew and that was how he planned on keeping it. It wasn't anyone's concern except his own. Liston tossed his shoes in the garbage bag. He trailed to the lobby of his restaurant and gazed out the front windows. Late afternoon sunlight filtered through the glass. He watched the dust in the air. The closed sign hung on the front door.

He was glad they closed early today. This wasn't even what he needed to be concerned with. Not today. There were other things on his mind, like his wife's surgery that had taken months to schedule. That was another thing he hated about Springdale. If you weren't dying, good luck being seen. Even then, it was hard to see a doctor. Hard to do anything medically related or find someone who cared.

Six months back, his wife found a small lump in her breast. After endless appointments and being ran around the loop, they'd finally decided that it was safest to remove it. A simple procedure, in and out. That's what they told them. Simple, but expensive. Their insurance covered most of it, but that only softened the blow.

Liston glanced at his phone. It was near 5:00 p.m. Francine's surgery had been scheduled for noon that day, but—of course—there'd been delays. The doctor not showing up on time. Getting caught up. God only knew, but he didn't.

She should've been done by now, but he hadn't gotten any word from her. He was originally supposed to pick her up at 5:15 p.m. The Meyer Center where her operation took place was maybe five minutes away. Ten in bad traffic. He hoped his wife was okay and that everything had gone well. She was what he needed to be worried about this afternoon, and not this bug shit.

Liston leaned on the front counter and sighed.

Seventeen years, he and Frankie had put into this joint. Seventeen hard years. Maybe it was time to move on. Find something else. Maybe the stress simply wasn't worth it anymore.

Outside the front windows, cars drug by on the main drag, back and forth, an endless stream. It didn't used to be like this. Not this many people. Not this much noise. He remembered when Springdale used to be a quiet town. A small town. Now, it was a decent sized city. Every day, it seemed to grow more and more, which had kept him in business, but had run him dry. For far too long, he'd burnt the candle on both ends. They both had—both him and Frankie—and he knew she was tired too, even if she never said anything to him. She was too much of a hard worker to ever say anything. A hell of a woman. He loved her more than anything.

Liston fished his keys out of his pocket and grabbed the garbage bag off the floor. He circled the front counter. Maybe it was time. If experience had taught him anything, it was that life was too short to waste any time, and the restaurant took up too much of it. Too much of his time. Too much of their life. Maybe it would be better to get up and move. Find another small town someplace else and start over. Find a quieter life, again.

His free hand twisted the deadbolt and he pushed

the door open. The pneumatic hinge wheezed behind him. The door closed and he twisted his key in the lock. He trailed around the side of the building, stepping over the river pebble that encircled the building. Out front, two round metal picnic tables with umbrellas stood sentry before the street. A single-lane drive-thru twisted around the building. The restaurant was small, but quaint.

His car sat parked around back. Liston stepped over the curb, into the lot and trailed to his vehicle. He thumbed the fob and hopped in the driver's. There was a lot to think about. Much to consider. But not right now. Right now, he only wanted to see his wife. He looked over his shoulder and backed out of his space.

At that moment, his only concern was seeing his wife, safe and healthy, and holding her in his arms, giving her a great big hug. He wanted to see Frankie, free and clear, and spend the evening with her, celebrating a successful surgery. Liston pushed all other concerns out of his mind. They were worries for tomorrow, but not for tonight. With only Frankie on his mind, he pulled out onto the street and drove to pick her up.

8

The phone kept ringing and hadn't stopped since noon, when he typically took his lunch break. Ever since it switched from a.m. to p.m. it seemed he'd been able to do nothing but pick up the phone, take down whatever details he needed, then place the receiver down, only to pick it right back up again. Every five minutes there'd been a call for him to come out and each call was for the same thing.

Wendell paced his back office, running his hand across his scalp, and pushing back what little hair he had that grew atop his head. He walked to his office chair and collapsed in it. His hand pulled out the desk drawer and reached into the open bag of Peanut M&M's, grabbing a fistful. He leaned over his desk and stared at his computer, popping pieces of candy in his mouth and crunching on them.

Tuesday, Wednesday, Thursday, and Friday were all booked. Calvin, Emory, Steven, and Garth were all on jobs, all day, for the rest of the week.

There was absolutely no room left. No where he could squeeze to fill in the gaps. There was no way to make anything else work. He glared at his excel sheet. There was no way he could. It was impossible. Since noon that day, he'd done nothing but contort every inch of his spreadsheet to make what he could work, but he'd reached his limit. There was nothing else he could do to extend his availability. He was booked clean out and that was that.

He reached into the bag of M&M's again, grasping blindly, only to come up with five of the candy-coated peanuts. He'd blown through the whole bag already. Wendell threw the remaining five into his mouth and slammed the drawer shut, standing from his desk. As he did, the phone on the cradle rang again. The registered name of the caller ran across the small digital face of the receiver. The time on his computer read 5:07 p.m. Wendell sent the call to voicemail. If they really needed him, they'd leave a message. If not, they'd go with a different business. Never in his life had he turned down business, but he couldn't take on any more. His capacity was capped. There was nothing else he could do.

He paced from his desk to the front lobby. On the counter, a pot sat on the coffee maker, that he brewed that morning. No one had come in.

There'd been no walk-ins. Just phone calls. Phone call after phone call. The whole office smelt of stale Folgers. In the corner of the room, the TV played on, babbling endlessly a stream of game shows. Wendell liked having it on for background noise. Sitcoms, gameshows. It didn't matter. Just as long as something was on that he could tune into. It acted as his white noise to help him get through the day. If not, the office was simply too quiet.

Wendell stood with his hands on his hips. His eyes rested on the television, watching the screen, but taking none of it in. A game show host consulted a giant screen to see what the survey said.

It was the damnedest thing, all of the calls. Every single one of them that day had been about roaches. Every call. Roaches in domiciles. Roaches in businesses. Roaches and roaches. Nothing else. No calls about bed bugs, mice, rodents, mosquitoes, racoons, skunks, squirrels or spiders. Only roaches. Yield comparison to some of the bigger companies in town, maybe he hadn't received that many calls, but for a one-man operation, there'd been more than he could handle and it was days like these that made him consider getting a secretary, though he couldn't afford it. Another paycheck, added to overhead and the team he already had simply wasn't feasible. Not when he could do the job himself. He couldn't justify paying someone to just sit and answer the phones all day.

These days came and went, he knew, but they stressed him out whenever they came. It always felt like this toward the end of the year. That's when his stress kicked into high gear. Every year was the same. Toward the end of the year, when it seemed everybody needed something from you, every minute, and when you were the only one who could provide it, that's when your stress levels peaked, and that's when Wendell's did the most.

It was because that's when everything came to a head. Everyone wanted off. Everyone wanted a bonus. Everyone wanted to know about the new year. It was when he promoted people, if the occasion rose. It was when he let go those that he didn't need anymore. Within the past five years, he'd actually hired five more men to join their team. The company was doing well, for just a ma and pa local business, but it'd been slow growing and tough in the making. He'd reared the company up from a two man operation, to a ten strong company that could accommodate almost any domestic or commercial job, but no matter how much his company had grown, it seemed that Springdale's needs had grown even quicker. He was constantly worried about staying afloat. Keeping new business growth, maintaining satisfied clientele, and trying to adapt to this new digital world, where everything was electronic. Everything was done online. In the world of pest control, he didn't see why it needed to be, but he'd done his best, hired people to establish, and then later clean up a website for his company. He did his homework and paid people and did what he was supposed to do. And it all cost money. The almighty dollar. That was what stressed him. Work and the almighty dollar that kept all afloat.

He sauntered to the front door and twisted the deadbolt. By the front window, he reached up and flicked the LED open sign off. Outside, the sun blazed on the horizon, just barely peeking over the line of buildings on the other side of the road.

The phone rang again behind him. Usually, if he was still in the office, he would pick it up. That was the expectation for his customers that he had created. One-on-one customer service. A handshake and a smile. Personalized, quality care. He knew his customers by name as they did him. So many aspects of the modern day didn't seem to give a good goddamn about that anymore. But there had to be a line in the sand.

He circled around the front counter and grabbed a tootsie roll from the bowl on the counter, next to their business cards. His fingers untwisted the wrapper and popped the chocolate in his mouth. The wrapper fell to the counter and his hands found their way to the bowl again, grabbing, unwrapping, and tossing another piece of candy into his mouth, without thought.

Call it a day, Wen.

The call went to voicemail and the machine behind him glowed as another message hit the inbox. He needed a break, but that wasn't in the cards. It seemed that what was in his cards were roaches. Bugs, bugs, bugs. Bugs, at least, for the rest of the foreseeable week. Then, maybe he could allot some time off. Maybe take off a day or two with the wife and kids and have a stay-cation. Maybe visit an amusement park. Relax. Not work. He needed a recharge, if nothing else. A break from wearing so many hats.

The sun fell behind the strip mall across the street and shadows filled the office. No lights were on. During the day, they weren't needed. The faint glow from the television filled the space with quivering light. His eyes fell to the counter. Between his arms, where he rested, a pile of candy wrappers laid discarded. Wendell sighed and crumpled them into a ball, tossing them into the trash behind the front desk. It was time to go home. He wanted to see his wife and end the day with a homecooked meal around the table with his family.

That was what all this was for, why it was worth it. Without them, none of it mattered.

Wendell went back to his office and grabbed his keys off his desk. From the back of his chair, he snagged his jacket. He loosened his tie as he came back up front. The remote to the TV sat on the counter. He pointed it at the box and clicked it off. Silence filled the office like water. Light ran from the space and shadows grew. The red light on the coffee maker shone in the dark. He went over and hit the button. Tomorrow, he'd toss it out and make a new pot. Not tonight.

In the dark, he shuffled to the front door, flicked open the deadbolt, and pushed outside. Shade from the veranda covered the entrance. It was getting darker earlier, now. Summer was coming to an end. That meant looking forward to cold weather again.

Wendell stepped to his car. He was parked right out front. As he keyed in, he caught his reflection in the driver's side window. He looked tired. Even to himself.

I'm getting old, he thought and dropped into the car.

There were things he didn't like about himself that he wished he could fix. His eyes flicked to the rearview mirror. He wished he wasn't balding like he was. He wished he wasn't gaining more weight each year, slowly packing on the pounds. He wished he didn't look and feel so damn tired all the time, but he didn't know exactly what to do. He just wanted to be more for his family. More for his wife. More for his kids.

Wendell backed of his space and switched the gear to drive. He pulled onto the street.

Home, James, home, he thought.

A small smile flickered on his face. That was all he needed to concern himself with. He cruised down Battlefield, coasting past green lights. As he got closer to home, the weight on his shoulders lifted. The thought of seeing his wife and kids grew steadily in his mind and by the time he pulled into his driveway, his worries faded to a whisper.

9

Nothing was going correctly and that seemed to be the trend for the day. Martin smacked his cell phone onto the counter. Absolutely absurd was what all of it was. Voicemail. Straight to voicemail. He checked the time. 5:07 p.m. That meant that someone had *sent* his call to voicemail. If no one was in the office, it would've kept ringing. If that was the case, he would've understood. It was believable—disappointing that everyone there would run out the door at exactly 5:00 p.m., but understandable, believable, sure—but after ringing once, the call went to the business's answering machine, meaning that someone had *sent* his call to voicemail. They hung up on him. His call wasn't not picked it up. It was ignored. Sent to voicemail. He couldn't believe it. What kind of way was that to run a business?

Martin hung up without recording a message. Never in his life had he dreamed of sending a customer to voicemail. Never in his life had he run out the door at 5:00 p.m. It was simply horrid customer service.

Martin leaned on the front desk and tapped his fingers, rhythmically on the stained wood. He'd have to call someone else tomorrow. Someone to take care of the problem. Bugs. Roaches, in the morgue. How morbidly ironic. His lip curled upward. Disgusting is what it was. He told Kent that they needed to get the place sprayed again.

"It's been some time since we had someone come out, Kent," he reminded him, but as per usual, his suggestions went unheeded. That was why they still had the awful green carpet decorating the lobby and why the wallpaper that was installed, back in 1986, when Kent started the business, was peeling from the walls. It was why the furniture had never been refurbished. It was why nothing in the funeral home had been updated or maintained at all. None of Martin's suggestions were ever considered and that was why the place was falling apart. It was why they were losing business. Neglect. Neglect, because Kent didn't want to adapt. He only wanted to do things the way they were always done. Simply put, Martin thought, he was stuck in the past and refused to move on.

The first real problem had come that morning, when the Kenleys arrived for visitation. At 10:00 a.m., they came to view the body before the visitation started and it was when they saw Mrs. Kenley in her casket that his troubles began.

"This isn't the dress we asked her to be put in," Leonara Baxter, the daughter had cried. She broke into tears when they entered the reception room. In front of the casket, she bent over and moaned when she saw the dress on her dead mother's body.

"She was supposed to be in her favorite floral dress, not this one," she wept. As she cried, her sisters flocked to her like a gaggle of geese from across the room. Then, all three began to cry, moaning, grabbing ahold of each other, wringing fistfuls of each other's dresses. They pulled tissue after tissue from small, leather clutches, slung over their shoulders and blew their noses as their makeup ran.

All three of their husbands tried to console them to no avail.

"Can't you people take simple instruction?!" Leonora turned, whipping from her husband, Frederick Baxter, to spit at him.

"Ma'am, these are the clothes we received to dress your mother in."

"Well, it's the wrong one!" she insisted.

Martin didn't argue. He simply waited for the moment to pass. Tears were dabbed, noses were wiped, and all three husbands did their best to soothe their wives before the visitation began.

Family members started arriving as the anger subsided. Soon, their attention turned fully to greeting mourners.

The second blow of the day came after the visitation. All went well during the initial proceedings. People congregated as Father Milton, from Segerman Baptist, spoke on life and death. He talked over the body of Peggy Cantor and words flowed eloquently from his lips to the small crowd before him of memories past. The father spoke of Peggy's commitment to her family and the community, to the church, and to all her friends, and how she would be missed by those around her, before inviting them all to bow their heads in prayer. The casket was closed and the body transported from the reception room to the funeral car. They exited the parlor, and Martin held the front door open for every family member to head for the cemetery. As the last family members passed into the parking lot, Leonora's husband, Frederick, grabbed him by the shoulder.

"Thank you for the service. I want to apologize for the outburst. This all has been hard for Lenny," he leaned in. His words slurred. Martin smelled stale whiskey, sour and thick, on his breath. As he exhaled, it hung in the air, sickly, cloying.

"It's quite alright," Martin smiled and pat him on the shoulder, ushering him along.

The other family members watched, nodding, smiling, tight mouthed. Peggy's casket was loaded into the coach. The last mourners exited the home and Martin locked the doors behind him. He got into the funeral car. The drive to Chestnut Memorial Gardens took only ten minutes. Traffic lights blessed him with green the entire way. Upon arriving, he maneuvered through the front gates and drove along the single lane road to the back of the cemetery. Peggy's plot sat near the rear, past the mausoleums up front. As he drove to the spot, he pulled past the looming crypts and parked, before stepping out and opening the coach.

Vehicles filed in, one at a time. All followed suit and the pallbearers came forth. Everyone grabbed a hold at the instruction of Martin, and at the golden opportunity of relocating Peggy's body one last time (over a distance of less than ten yards) when they lifted the casket, calamity struck. Two bearers lost their grip and the casket dropped. The lid bounced up as it hit the grass. Peggy's arm flopped out and caught in between. The Cantor sisters went into hysterics. Many gasped. Children cried and Frederick Baxter—who Martin knew had been one of the bearers that dropped the coffin—spurted out *"Goddammit!"* drawing eyes to himself.

Without a moment's hesitation, Martin tucked

Peggy's arm back in her casket and roused the men standing around the coffin, staring down at it, to resume their duties and finish carrying the body to the grave. Ignoring the sobs from Leonora and her sisters, the men, minus Frederick, transported the casket to the top of the lowering device. Then, they all stood back and Father Milton, flustered and red in the face (a witness to the entire debacle, from off on the sidelines), came forth and ran through the closing remarks to conclude their service.

No one lingered by the grave.

When Martin got back to the funeral home, exhaustion swept him. There were no more scheduled funerals for the day, nor any shipments, deliveries—nothing. Upon arriving back in the lobby, he locked the front doors behind him, walked over to the couch, and plopped himself down. He laid his head back and closed his eyes, planning to only rest, laying down for just a minute. When his eyes opened again, he had slept for two hours. The clock behind the front desk read 3:37 p.m. He cupped his face in his palms. Days like these exhausted him.

He pushed himself up and walked to the blue door that led to the back and the preparation room. There were several bodies that needed final touches for services tomorrow. He treaded past the minister's room and down the hall to the entry door. Since there was no basement in the building, the preparation room was located in the far rear of the building, apart from everything. Martin figured the design must have been intentional, to make it a longer trip for wandering visitors to accidentally stumble into the workspace and see a body in the middle of embalming. A smile rose to his face as he shouldered into the room. The thought of a nosy little child traumatizing themselves with the sight of a body being worked on tickled him, especially considering all the children he'd dealt with over the years. Most were well-behaved, somber visitors, but some had no respect, nor understanding of the funerals they'd been a part of. Disrespect inherently bothered Martin.

His feet tramped from carpet to epoxy flooring. He hit the light switch, bathing the room in LED white, and the third misfortune struck that day as the door closed behind him. His smile tore from his lips. He stared in silence at the middle of the room. Atop the stainless-steel embalming table, a bug skittered, then froze. Under the glow of the lights, it held still, its antennae twitching. Martin glared at the bug.

He looked around the room for anything to kill it with and when he turned his head, the insect darted. The small shape twisted under the table and Martin lost it. He dropped to his knees and looked, but found nothing. For the next hour, he moved everything in the preparation room, trying to find the bug. He shifted equipment, moved cabinets, pulled out chairs, lifted boxes, all to no avail. Where there was one, there were likely more, and he couldn't even find where this one went.

What a lovely cap to the day, he thought.

When he picked up his phone to dial an exterminator, he saw it was nearly 5:00 p.m. His fingers tapped on his cellphone, searching for anyone near them to come out. He scrolled through businesses and settled on the first one that popped up. Good ratings. Decent reviews. Martin stormed out of the preparation room, back to the lobby. Sweat ran down the middle of his back. Beads formed on his forehead. His breath hissed in and out of his clenched teeth. As he phoned the business, he tried relaxing his jaw. Under stress, he always ground his teeth.

The phone rang once, then went straight to voicemail.

"Unbelievable," he said. His palm slammed down, slapping the phone on the counter. By now, an almost full sweat had broken out over his body. The back of his shirt clung to him under his jacket. Foolish, foolish, foolish. He didn't know why Kent couldn't've just had the godforsaken motivation to keep the place in proper running order. Martin felt as if he ran the entire facility by himself. He might as well have owned it, for everything he did to keep operations running smoothly.

When it rains, it assuredly pours, he thought and stared across the front lobby. His hand crawled to his phone and picked it up. He listlessly scrolled through the other exterminators around town. All of them were closed, now. Past five, nothing of the sort was open. It would have to wait until tomorrow. Another problem for him to dwell upon and think about. Just wonderful. It was always something. Always something wrong. Same shit, different day. Goodness.

Martin tapped his fingers on the counter. His teeth clenched together, his molars sliding back and forth, back and forth. Tomorrow. Tomorrow. First thing tomorrow, he would come in, finish up what he needed to do, and call the exterminator as soon as they opened up. He would come in early, get done what needed to be, with plenty of time to spare, and have the rest of the day to see to his tasks, without feeling any of the rush that he felt today—without any of the stress. Yet, he knew that as soon as he emptied his bucket, it would only fill immediately, again.

Never mind. Martin stamped his foot on the carpet, then turned and paced to the preparation room again. He flicked off the light in the space, closed the door behind himself, and tramped back to the lobby. His keys jangled in pocket. He turned around, surveying the room. Everything was off. All the lights. All was put away.

"Okay," he said to no one, and pushed through the front doors into the late afternoon warmth. Sunlight filtered between the leaves of the oak trees before the building. Warmth lapped at his skin. Tomorrow, he would take care of it all, but not this evening. This evening, what he had to look forward to was whatever he planned, and at that moment, a large glass of chardonnay and a bath seemed to be calling his name. Relaxation and not a care in the world. The problems were for another day. You simply had to know when to call it good for the day, and when to cut yourself off.

Martin fished his keys from his pocket, walking across the lot to his car. He slid into the driver's seat. Yes, a glass of Josh and possibly some cheese and crackers would do quite nicely. His hand twisted his key in the ignition. The engine rumbled to life and he pulled out of his spot.

Tomorrow, tomorrow, and tomorrow.

Bugs, he thought. *Push it out of your mind.*

His car rolled to the edge of the street. He turned left and drove. Sometimes, after a long day, it was as simple as a glass of wine and a relaxing tub to ease the nerves, and Martin had just that plan in mind. Nothing else. Not today. Tomorrow, and tomorrow, and tomorrow. From that point forward, it was all about himself. He felt no qualms about it, no grief in letting it go. Tomorrow's problems were tomorrow's. They were worries for another day, something he could think about later, and he had absolutely no problem with that. No problem at all. He'd dealt with enough for the day.

10

Jon peeked over the lip of the grave. He'd dug the hole about five feet deep already. The cavity only needed another foot in depth to accommodate the casket. The width and length were already accounted for: 3' x 8'. He squinted at the sun, bleeding over the edge. It was going to get dark soon. He needed to hurry up and finish.

It'd been an early day—a busy day—and he was tired and wanted to go home. He dug his spade into the fresh dirt. It cut into the earth, slicing through it. Jon heaped it full and tossed it over his shoulder. To his right, a small mound stood watching over him, a dark outline. Shadows stretched over the mouth of the grave. Above him, light faded from the sky, grew deeper, and sweltered.

He glanced at his watch. On his wrist, the small electronic face read 6:46 p.m. It was getting darker earlier and earlier. Summer was over, fall arrived, and daylight savings was soon to be leaving. The days grew shorter. Jon always hated the changing of the seasons. He hated seeing the leaves fall from the trees, seeing the grass grow yellow and withered, the look of barren tree limbs reaching out. Most of all though, he hated the cold. The unfeeling, gray, cold. He hated the cold December ushered, and that remained throughout January, February, and March, like a wet, smothering blanket. He hated the death of everything and the frigid numbness that took hold.

When he was a child, he lived in Florida and fondly remembered the ever-present warmth that existed there. The status of season. Warmth never left. Granted, there were no leaves changing, no seasons, but it was always warm, never cold. Never bitter. Never biting. He'd grown tired of harsh winters. Scraping windshields, constantly being cold, not wanting to go outside because it was damp and freezing, wanting only to stay inside and bundle up. It stole your joy, the cold, the wet. The unforgiving wind that flayed your skin. The black ice. The loss of light. The loss of daylight. The loss of sun. The loss of warmth. It got to you over time.

It'd been too long that he dealt with it all. Suicide weather. That was his name for it, because for those three months, it was easy to get the blues. It was easy to get in a bad headspace and hard to get out of. It was the damn cold.

Jon lugged another shovel full of dirt over his shoulder and it landed with a thwunk atop the pile. He wanted to move. He wanted to for a long time, but family kept him there. Now there was no one. Not anymore.

His father was diagnosed with Parkinson's a decade earlier. For most of his adult life, he watched his father deteriorate, until he couldn't take care of himself anymore, so Jon moved in with him. His mother passed away years before, as had both of his grandparents, so when his father needed help, he was the only one. No one else, really, kept in touch. Jon's father never wanted to go into a facility. That had been his one request to his son, so Jon took care of him. His condition worsened over time, so Jon learned to feed, bathe, and change his father. Eventually, taking care of him became like taking care of a child—synonymous with caring for a toddler—and Jon saw the pain in his father's eyes every day. He took care of him until the end. A massive stroke took him in five minutes. Jon had been there when it happened and watched his father die as he talked to the dispatch officer.

That was four years ago. That same year, he sold his father's house. After everything, he couldn't stand to live in the home, so he sold it, placed the money in savings, and rented an apartment in town. He took care of everything that his father left undone and then sat. A sense of creeping unknowing took over his life. For so long, he existed in a routine. A void was left when his father died. Looking back, he knew it was a blessing that his father's death came so quickly, but he often wondered why it didn't come sooner and asked, *what was the point of all the needless suffering?*

Jon shoveled dirt out of the hole. There was nothing here for him anymore.

So, why are you here? Why are you wasting time?

He couldn't answer that. He didn't know.

That morning, driving into work, he saw a hit deer, and the image stuck with him. It'd been toward the end of his drive, at the intersection of Battlefield and Lone Pine, where the road sloped downhill. For the hundred or so yards where woods enclosed both sides of the road until it intersected at the light, halfway down the hill, Jon saw the deer. It'd been in the left hand lane on the opposite side. Someone had hit it and he caught a glimpse, zooming by, headed to work. It'd been alive and showed no obvious signs of injury. There'd been no blood, nor gore to speak of. Only the deer lying on its side, in the middle of the lane. When he passed by, the deer had been seizing uncontrollably. Its head twitched, slamming against the pavement and its eyes glazed over, wide in their sockets. Jon only saw the deer for a fraction of a second, but he'd met its eyes. In them, he saw the same pain he saw in his father's.

For every deer he passed that'd been hit, on the side of the road, none ever bothered him. The messes that made him look away or change lanes to avoid driving over, never affected him. None ever bothered him, but that morning, when he met the deer's eyes, it stayed with him because it was still alive and suffering, and he could do nothing about it.

Jon looked at his feet and couldn't see them. Outside the grave, the sun had set. Darkness fell upon the cemetery. He leaned his shovel against the dirt wall and grabbed his flashlight. His eyes scaled the depth of the hole, top to bottom. It looked deep enough now. The beam doused the bottom of the grave, searching for his footstool. He found it and folded it out. One foot, then the other, he climbed atop it and set his flashlight by the lip of the grave. Both of his hands planted down and he boosted himself out.

Cool air rushed him as he stepped back onto level earth. The cemetery extended, a shadowland, around him. No one remained except for him. To the side of the road, his truck waited for him. Tomorrow morning was the scheduled funeral for Mr. Stout. This was where they would bury him.

In the grave he dug that evening. Jon looked at the rectangle in the ground he carved out and the pile of dirt beside it. He breathed in deeply and sighed.

There was too much death. Too much hurt. He dropped to his knees and fished the stool and shovel out of the grave. Meaningless hurt. It didn't make sense. He grabbed his flashlight off the ground and came to a stand. Dirt caked the front of his jeans. Nothing made much sense. Not here, at least. Not anymore. Jon brushed himself off.

In the closet at home, he kept a small safe on the floor. In the safe was a letter he had written four months ago, detailing his resignation from the groundskeeper position. It thanked Hermann-Kopf Funeral Home for their kindness and loyalty to him over the years and in few words expressed his regret. On the front of the envelope, small, black-inked script addressed the letter to Kent Overholt, the home's director.

The rent on his apartment was paid monthly, and his possessions were few and far between. It would take only an hour to load everything into his truck. Yesterday, he even filled up the tank when he got paid. From his apartment, the drive to Hermann-Kopf took nine minutes.

Jon felt his keys in his pocket and walked to his truck. It didn't seem there was much else to do, much else to decide.

So, why are you here?

As he piled into his truck, his hand pushed the key into the ignition for him. The engine twisted alive.

"I don't know," he said to the empty cab. The gear shifted to drive and he pulled forward out. His words echoed in his ears across the ride home and when he pulled into his apartment's parking lot, they still rang. When he opened his truck door, he had an answer. An hour later, the letter was dropped off.

11

There was something there was something there was something there was something there was something.

Ralph stopped, his spade in the dirt, and became motionless in the hole he'd dug. There was something. He heard something, heard something, heard something. There was something there, something there, something there, something there.

His ears perked. From beyond the grave, something moved. A crunching noise. The sound of feet over dead leaves. Walking. Moving. Someone else. Someone else someone else someone else someone else. His lips split apart in a grin. He ceased movement entirely. No one would hear him, no one would hear him, no one would hear him if he didn't move. The feet moved—moved, moved, moved—closer to him. Closer to the road. He heard a whispered jangle. Something tinkle. Metal. Keys. Then gnashing gravel. Boots stepped. One after the other one after the other. Getting closer. The boots stepped and his lips pulled further apart, exposing his teeth. His hands shook by his side. His head tilted. He listened to the interrupter. The interrupter, interrupter, interrupter, interruuuuuuuuupter. Interrupting his work. Interrupting his scrounge. His dive, his dive. His dive deep into the grave, into the graveyard, into the scrounge. Into his scrouuuuunge. The footsteps moved closer, alongside the road.

Ralph leaned against the cool dirt wall of the grave. His head throbbed. He let go of the shovel. Blood pulsed in his temples. Both of his eyes felt like hot marbles. He looked ahead at nothing and lost all focus to his ears, the blood flowing in them, the footsteps by the road. Thwomp thwomp, thwomp thwomp, thwomp thwomp, thwomp thwomp. He listened to the crunching gravel, the moving man, and his hand crept into the pocket of his jeans and grabbed, grabbed. In the depth of his overalls, he found his blade and stroked the edge, back and forth. His pointer finger rubbed along the tip, listening to the steps. The blade slit his skin. Blood trickled from his finger. He grabbed the shaft of the knife and his breath deepened. If the steps came closer, if the steps came closer, came closer, came closer, came, came, came, came. He gripped the knife's handle as the steps grew louder, approaching his hole, his work, his scrounge.

The dirt felt gooooooooood against the side of his head. He sucked air in. His lips trembled. The footsteps stopped. A door opened. Shut again. Then silence. Dead air. His eyes shifted and looked upward. Nothing moved. Everything, quiet. Wind blew through the trees. The low growl of traffic came from nearby roads. An engine roared to life. The air shattered like glass. Gravel crunched and the vehicle rolled away. The engine diminished. Gone, gone, gone. It faded, quieter, quieter, quiet, quiet, quiet, until he couldn't hear it.

Ralph's eyes rolled back to the grave. Back to his scrounge. Back back back get back get back get back. His hand let go of the blade. He grabbed the shovel and stabbed at the dirt. The spade struck hard and sweet vibrations shook up his arm. There was something, he reached something reached something reached something. His mind flooded with waves of ecstasy. Thoughts of feeeeling, good feelings, good feeeeeeling ran up his spine. Thoughts of the coffin. Thoughts of insiiiiiiiiide. Thoughts of flesh. Feeling flesh. Feeling the body. Spit ran from his mouth and dripped down his chin.

He dropped to his hands and knees and felt at the dirt. His fingers dug, scraped, scratched. The curvature of a casket lid appeared and shined in the dark, polished, metallic, beautiful. Shiny like coins, like coins, his treasure, his treasure, his treasure, his treasure, his scrouuuunnnggee. He laid against the lid and felt for the lip. Dirt pressed against his cheek. He lunged for the crowbar and jammed it into the earth, once, twice, three times, again, again. Metal scraped metal, bounced off, jammed. Sweat dripped down his body, slicking his hair to his forehead. He brought the crowbar down again, again, again. It sunk and connected, lodging into the crack. He got to his feet and leaned all his weight against the lever. The casket moaned in protest and he jimmied the crowbar further in. His muscles corded. Dirt shifted. The lid creaked up and he grabbed the shovel. He jammed the spade into the narrow opening, shoving it upward. The opening grew and he gripped underneath. Cloth interior rubbed against his palms. Pain splintered up his finger, gripping the lid. From the pressure, fresh blood pumped and seeped down his wrist; a thin, warm rivulet.

The lid screeched, then fell open. A plume of smell, a thick warm cloud sifted up to him. Fresh. Ripe. Old. Decayed. The sweet, sweet smell of rot, rot, rot, rot, rot. From the shadows, an eyeless corpse looked up at him. He stood above the body, both feet planted to each side of the coffin. Below him, the woman laid among tattered velvet.

Patches of skin clung to her skeleton. A tethered dress hugged her form. No lips covered her teeth, no gums surrounded them. Thin whisps of hair draped down her shoulders. Fragments of scalp stuck to her skull. On her neck hung two golden necklaces. On her wrists, two bracelets.

Ralph lowered himself into the casket with her and pressed his body against hers. He grabbed her hand and lifted it before his eyes. Rings adorned the pinky and ring. Gold with stones. They glinted in the moonlight. He bit his lip and sat back on the skeleton. A smile rose to his face as he raised the hand before him, looking at the them. His treasure, his scrounge, his scrounge, his scrooouuunnngge. His left hand wrapped around the wrist and the other gripped the first finger and twisted. The digit snapped off, and he broke off the second, letting them fall into the grave. He dropped the hand back beside the corpse. His eyes came alive as he held the rings up in the moonlight. Both of them gleamed in the pale lighting, the barren night. The stones both gleamed, gleamed, shiiiiiinnnnned. He tucked the rings in the pocket of his overalls and shot his hands out, grabbing the necklace. The body lifted as he tore at the jewelry, before the latch broke and came free in his fists and the body fell. Shining, shining, shining, shining. His eyes moved to the bracelet. He shoved the necklace with the rings and snatched at the corpse's wrists. In his grip, the skin rubbed, moved over the bone, loose, loose, loose, smooooth. He rubbed the bone that poked out from underneath, twisted the hand in his own, and broke it free from the skeletal wrist. The bracelet slid off and he shoved it in his pocket.

He leaned down against the body and smiled. His hand ran over the corpse's chest. He felt each rib of the ribcage, rib, rib, rib, each peak and valley, up and down. The front of his denim stiffened against him. Spit slicked his lips. His treasure, treasure, treasure, treasure, treasure, treasuuuuuree. He pressed his hand against the corpse's sternum and lowered his mouth to the exposed grin of the body. The bone-white smile. The teeth, the teeth. His tongue slipped from his mouth and ran over the front canines. Beneath his weight, the sternum pressed inward, flexed, and he wedged his tongue between the teeth, pushing them apart, as the ribcage collapsed. Pain stabbed into his hand as the bone broke and stabbed into his palm. He lifted himself up and looked at his hand, but the pain felt good, good, good, good, good and more warmth ran down his arm as he raised it above him and watched the blood flow. It looked black against his skin. His eyes turned back to his scrouuuuuunnnggge. He placed his bloodied hand against the cool dirt wall of the grave and began to lower himself again when the body wheezed.

Air exhaled. The mouth opened wider. Beneath the body, the earth shifted and he watched it push up around the bones. The body began to sink. Dirt swallowed the broken ribcage, the sternum, the spine, then pushed out of the mouth and sept from the eyes. The grave was sinking.

Ralph pushed himself back, away from the body. He watched as the dirt swallowed the bones, before rising toward his feet. The dirt covered them. His eyes squinted and pain erupted over his skin as the dirt crawled up his ankles, swarming his legs. Thousands of shells glittered in the moonlight. The ground beneath him writhed and squirmed. A scream tore from his lips.

He turned and clawed at the edge of the grave. The tide swelled into his pant legs, up his thighs, past his waist, and agony hijacked his senses. Warmth flowed from every pore. Broken glass burrowed into him. Fiberglass shards slithered into his body.

His fingers dug into the grass surrounding the grave. Cold dirt shoved under his fingernails. His feet kicked beneath him, trying to push himself out. The pain rose up his chest, past his neck, to his head and he couldn't feel his legs. His fingers sunk in dirt. His vision left him and his arms became detached, phantom limbs. His mouth opened to scream and the pain tore into his jaw. His throat swelled with the skittering tide. His body seized, then ceased moving, all except the covering of shells, consuming it. Near silence rose again and no sound came from the grave except a chittering whisper, subdued scuttling. As the breeze blew through the graveyard, the sound was lost. No one heard and no one saw. The pulsing body sunk back into the grave and the night crept on, unknowing and blind.

12

The scenery passed him in a blur. Buildings flowed by, meaningless imagery. Even his thoughts flew away from him. Slight turns let the wheel decide on its own where to go. He directed the car only minimally—allowing an automatism to his steering— and found his way onto 60, then out of town, without second thought. It was getting late already. If he didn't turn back, it'd be even later by the time he got home. He'd be tired tomorrow for work if he didn't stop.

If, if, if.

Matthew swiped all concerns away. He let them fly away from him, let them go, swatted them from his mind and pressed his foot down on the pedal listening to only the drowning noise of the wind. But still, the thoughts came like swarming mosquitoes.

You need to think. You need to do something, a voice inside urged, though he couldn't name it.

He was depressed, tired and depressed, tired of

what he was doing, but unsure of what to do next. Dissatisfaction dominated his life and underneath it all, he was terrified of giving up. Every day, going into work, dealing with the same people, smiling, shaking hands, and selling, constantly selling, exhausted him. No satisfaction came from it. Customer service. He was twenty-nine years old and couldn't imagine sticking it out for another thirty-one years. Merely waiting it out. Toughing it out. When life became like that, you were no longer living. When wrung dry, simply counting the days, wishing them away, that wasn't life. That was merely existing, and that was what Matthew was afraid of. Nothing inspired him in his current position and though it was comfortable, he hated it. It couldn't go on. For so long, he kept up the façade, but the gig was up, the muse was out, and he couldn't keep it up anymore. The time had come, but he had no plan. With the new house, he had payments to make.

But you had payments to make when you were living in an apartment.

And there was the possible promotion to consider.

But it's not guaranteed, and what difference would it make?

More money.

More stress. More of the same stress. More hours.

More frustration. More obligations.

If he kept moving up, he could get a job elsewhere. Mr. Ordner told him that they were planning on opening a new storefront in Arkansas, and the original plan had been to wait until the end of the year, collect his bonus and see if anything changed on that front, but everyday it only got worse. He couldn't fake caring anymore and he was afraid someone soon was going to catch on. It hurt every day to wear a fake smile, act like all was okay, laugh and joke, make small talk with customers who really didn't give a shit how he was. It hurt to spin his wheels, day after day, busting his butt and working after hours, coming in on the weekends, staying late, coming in early, being willing to uproot his entire life to move up in the company, because now he was tired and the question arose: did he even want it if it was offered to him? Did any promotion or raise or relocation even matter?

"You've got a hell of a future, here, Matt," his boss told him before they all left on Christmas Eve. He got a single day off to visit his family. "I got big plans for you," Mr. Ordner told him, and he believed that, but did he want it?

The answer was no, in the end, but no one knew that. Not yet.

He didn't want to be like Mr. Ordner with the

company. Tenured, comfortable, happy, waiting, spending more time at work than he ever did at home. He didn't want to die inside to achieve financial security. He didn't want the work he hated to become his life. He didn't want it to drain him. He wanted more from life, surely there had to be more, because if going to work every day from 9:00 am to 7:00 pm and coming home too tired to do anything, week after week, month after month—if that's all there was to life, then he wanted out.

There had to be more. That couldn't be it. He knew there was more, but he couldn't walk just away. It wasn't as simple as that. It wasn't a matter of quitting and starting anew.

Maybe it is as simple as that.

He had to be smart, though.

But maybe that's the first step.

Throwing away his bright future there, wasting his potential.

Maybe making what so many others would consider a stupid decision is what you need to do.

There was truth to that. Hard truth to that singular decision. Throwing away a future.

The sun set and his wheels rotated beneath him, pulling him down the highway. Miles grew between him and his house.

A house doesn't make a home.

He pursued the endless road, searching for nothing.

What if you never stopped? What if you just kept going? What if you drove until you ran out of gas, then stopped at the nearest motel and stayed there? What if you didn't come back? What if you didn't show up to work tomorrow? What if you just left? What if you left it all?

The fact that that wasn't an option gritted him inside. The fact that he was stuck.

But are you really stuck? Are you really trapped?

He couldn't simply leave.

But you could sell the house. You could sell the house and leave your job. You could make gradual changes. You could leave if you wanted to.

And that was true. Gradual changes. Gradual changes he could make, toward betterment, toward something else, something new, something he enjoyed.

He didn't want to think about these things, but the thoughts came regardless. Prodding questions that demanded answers. They always arose when he needed to think and didn't want to. The hardest thinking was always the kind he never wanted to do. Change came gradually and there was always resistance because it required work, and hard work at that. Change was necessary though because he couldn't maintain his situation. The situation he existed in no longer remained tenable. He had to change. Something had to change.

The horizon flattened to both sides of his car as he moved further from the city and into the no-man's-land boonies that surrounded Springdale. BFE, his father always called it. Bum-fuck Egypt. BFE dominated the landscape. Bales of hay, wrapped in white, dotted extending fields. Barbed wire fences marked properties. Cattle grazed. The road climbed and dove, following rolling hills, curving back and forth. Countryside stretched endless miles.

Matthew's automatic lights clicked on as shadows grew and the sun fell further from the sky. Trees turned to shadow puppets to his left and right. Behind them, the sky blended from sherbert orange to mellow blue. A rich ombré stain blurred the skyline as light faded and night set. Cars became sparse as he drove on.

His stomach growled beneath his shirt. He hadn't had anything to eat since lunch, around noon, and now he was feeling it. Exhaustion hung on his shoulders. His back felt stiff, and ready to pop. The wind rushing through the car took on a chill as the warmth left the day. He rolled up the windows, then closed the sunroof. Everything sealed and silence whooshed into the cab.

The radio fizzled, crackling out of reception.

Matthew hit the last preset, changed the channel, and another station came through clearer with an advertisement for getting out of timeshares. A reporter came on giving the rundown of tomorrow's weather. The news subsided and a disc jockey took control, spieling off an event he was working that week, before introducing a song. Music ambled from the speakers.

If he kept going straight, he'd reach Willow Springs before he knew it. His speedometer read seventy. He hit cruise control and took his foot off the pedal. A road sign passed by indicating 92 miles to Ellington. In the right hand lane, he came up behind a silver Honda and switched into the left to pass by it. His blinker clicked. He flipped it off, then toggled it right to switch back into the slow lane. The groan in his stomach subsided. On his dash, the gauge read that he still had half a tank. Plenty of miles to burn until he ran empty. His eyes sank back into the road and he let himself float, mindless again.

The radio played and the asphalt stretched. Soon, his car became the only one that he could see for miles. His headlights illuminated the highway before him. The dashed road divider blurred into a continuous line. He sank into his seat and his hands rested on the wheel. All became periphery and he simply drove.

13

"And our twentieth player who will be proceeding to the second round of the tournament tomorrow is..." the announcer paused behind her microphone, eyes scanning the crowd, building anticipation, "Miss Mary Joan from Polk County," she relented and a round of applause ran over the audience.

Her heart soared. She already knew that she was moving on. That evening she played five games and won every one of them. She'd been surprised at the range of contestants. Players from all over Missouri had come to the event, young and old, men and women, and many different ethnicities. She couldn't believe it. She'd played two older women her age, a younger fellow named Jim, and two middle aged ladies, who just so happened to be neighbors: Pam and Matty. There'd been a few close games, but she won every one of them, but it wasn't until hearing her own name, that it became real. At the confirmation, her heart soared. She was moving on to the next rounds. That meant she had to be up early tomorrow to be at the convention center in time, again.

And this time, I'll know where I'm going, she thought. While competing, she made a new friend, and one that was moving on with her, at that.

Her new friend's name was Rose. She was ninety-one and also widowed, she had the most gorgeous smile Mary had ever seen, and she was a hugger. After playing two rounds that evening, Mary met Rose when she went to the ladies' room. Rose started up a conversation while they were washing their hands before leaving.

"Young lady, that is the most beautiful dress I've ever seen," she said to Mary. Mary blushed and complimented her back, mousing that the straw-hat Rose was wearing was the most splendid hat she'd ever seen.

The two conversed as they left the bathroom and chatted for their entire break between rounds. Mary relayed to her how she walked to the convention center and got lost on the way. Rose laughed and told Mary how she had done the same thing, and how she thought she wasn't going to make it in time until some nice young man stopped off the street and guided her there himself.

"There are still good people in the world," Rose enunciated each syllable with a tapping finger on

Mary's shoulder. "I do believe that."

"As do I," Mary said.

The timer went off as they both smiled at one another, cutting their conversation right at a break in words. Before departing, Rose invited Mary to ride with her and her friend Edith back to the Marriott when that night's rounds were said and done. Mary agreed and thanked her.

"I wish you the best of luck," Rose said and caught her in a vice grip of a hug, surprising Mary. Her breath puffed from her chest. For such an old lady, she hugged like a bear. Mary wrapped her arms around Rose and hugged her back.

"I wish you all the same, Rose."

Two hours later, both their names were called as part of the twenty moving on. After tomorrow, there would only be ten. That evening, they had started with over one hundred contestants; now, she was one of the twenty moving on.

Eighty people, Mary Joan. You beat out eighty others.
So did Rose.

"Mary Joan!" she called from across the room, as the announcer relayed the time tomorrow's matches would begin and how excited they were to see the faces of that evening's winners there again in the morning. "It looks like we're both moving on, girlie!" Rose said as she shuffled to Mary, dancing across the patterned carpet floor.

Another older woman followed behind her.

For an older gal, she sure can dance, she thought, and made her way past the rows of tables and chairs. *I only hope to have as much spit and grit as she does when I reach her age.* The thought brought a smile to her face that only grew when Rose met her in another hug.

"You still want a ride home with this old gal?" she said, looking up to meet her eyes, and Mary's widened in one-sided shock. It was as if she read her mind and pulled the thought right out of her head. Rose winked at her, as if knowing.

"I would be honored," she said. "This must be Edith, then," Mary said and extended her hand to shake to the woman beside Rose.

"Oh hell, it's Eddie honey, and I'm a hugger too," the older woman swatted Mary's hand out of the air and hugged the two women together. The three of them wrapped their arms around one another in the convention room, squeezed tight, then let go and stood back. They all looked at one another and laughed.

"What an evening!" Eddie said. A silk scarf tied her flowing white hair back. Piercing green eyes shined from her wrinkled face. She was old, but beautiful.

"What an evening," Mary agreed and met Eddie's eyes, dazzling, wonderful. There was a life in them that was missing from so many others she had seen. A vivacity that glowed and emanated from each. To Mary Joan, she looked more alive than most others.

That's what joy looks like, Mary blushed, before forcing herself to turn away. *That's a content heart*, she thought as she looked to Rose.

"Shall we?" Rose asked, and the two ladies nodded their affirmations before they all took off.

Out in the back parking, Eddie whipped out her keys from her purse and thumbed the fob, starting up a shining white Cadillac from across the lot. The vehicle purred to life and its lights came on.

"Howya like that?" Eddie said and smiled. "Can start the damn thing up without even being in it!"

She laughed and the sound of her laughter caused the other two ladies to join in with her. It was infectious. Warm, welcoming, mellow. A toast to life. That's what the evening felt like.

The three piled into Eddie's car. Rose and Mary giggled watching in admiration as Eddie climbed into the driver's and sat behind the gigantic wheel. Then, they fell about each other, laughter turning to outright, uncontrolled guffawing, as they struggled themselves to climb the side of the ginormous vehicle. Eventually, the two made it inside. Mary in the back middle and Rose in the front passenger. All three of their stomachs ached from laughter and their brows grew damp with sweat.

The drive back to the Marriot wrought no less joy. Eddie whipped her boat-of-a-vehicle around downtown. She drove it like she stole it. While on any other occasion it would have made Mary nervous, that night she laughed at every stop sign Eddie almost missed as she barked the brakes and said "Oops!" before giggling. Mary felt seventeen again. The trip called back memories of riding home with her high school friends. Wild and free, warm recollections percolated her thoughts of summer nights. Summer nights backroading in the country, the radio on full blast, high on life. Full of joy. Full of life. Not tired and worn. Unaged. Untouched.

That was how she felt that afternoon and now this evening. This was living. Her smile stayed for the entire ride back and didn't leave when they left the vehicle.

When they pulled into the parking lot, Eddie screamed.

"Sweet deedums! Butter me up and call me a biscuit, hot damn!" She veered the Cadillac to skid into a front row spot. "Thank you God, thank you Jesus, for doing the things which all'a please us!"

The trio left the vehicle in hysterics and were met by a young front receptionist on the way in. As the doors slid open before them and they entered the hotel, a young Hispanic man called from behind the front desk.

"Miss Eddie, Miss Rose, it's a pleasure to see you both again."

The young man wore a gleaming white smile. Thick, rich dark hair ran in waves from his head. A suit and tie served as his uniform.

"Spiffy and good lookin'", Mary surprised herself when she quipped, as she followed Eddie and Rose to the front desk.

"How did the competition go this evening?" he asked as the three women approached the counter.

"We're movin' on, Danny," Eddie said, and the man looked to Rose, who nodded in confirmation.

"Well, congratulations. And is this a friend you made this evening?" he asked as he extended a hand across the granite countertop.

"Sure is," Eddie answered.

Mary took his hand and shook it. "Mary," she said. "It's a pleasure to meet you, Danny."

"The pleasure is all mine," he said and kissed the top of her hand, setting Mary's cheeks afire.

My goodness! Was all she could think. Mary took her hand back, coyly.

"Quit flirtin', Danny, we're too old for you!" Eddie swatted at his hand, like shooing away a fly.

"Well, he can flirt with me all he likes," Rose said

quietly. Eddie and Mary both looked at her, before falling into laughter again.

In the corner of the lobby, an older man squinting at his phone, craned his neck up and made a face at the noise. Danny noticed and leaned in.

"Well, if there's anything I can do for you lovely ladies tonight, just let me know, and I'll be right there."

I can think of a few things, Mary thought, and once again, her face flushed with heat. *Mary Joan, you stop that*. A smile spread wide on her lips and she giggled to herself. Her ears flared red.

Eddie noticed, then hooked her and Rose by the arms. "Well, I'd better get these two to their rooms, Danny. I'll tell you, it's hard work being the responsible one in our group."

That sent them all into laughter again, but Eddie succeeded in guiding them all to the elevator doors. Eddie pressed the *UP* button and the elevator dinged down to the first. The doors slid open, they all stepped in, and Danny waved goodbye as the doors slid shut.

"What floor you on, sweetcheeks?" Eddie looked to Mary and asked.

"Floor six."

Eddie thumbed the button and the elevator ascended. They arrived at the sixth floor, the doors slid open, and Mary stepped out.

"Goodnight Mary," Rose said. "We'll see you bright and early first thing tomorrow."

"Wanna have breakfast with these old gals?" Eddie asked.

Mary nodded and the doors started to slide closed. Eddie thwacked the open button and they reversed.

"That would be wonderful," Mary said.

"What's your room number?" Eddie asked as the doors started to slide shut again.

"604."

"We'll come get you in the morning. See you at eight," Eddie smiled and winked as the elevator closed. The car dinged up to the 7th, 8th, 9th, 10th floor, and Mary chuckled to herself as she turned to face the hall. Her shoes padded over the carpet as she walked down the silent corridor to her room. A friendly aroma hung in the air. Some air freshener plugged in somewhere, but it smelled nice. Nothing artificial and sickening. The aroma reminded her of freshly washed linen.

Mary dug in her clutch for her keycard. As she arrived at her door, she scanned the sensor and beeped into her room. The door whooshed closed behind her. Her hand fumbled blindly for the light switch and found it. She flipped it, illuminating the room, then turned the deadbolt on the door and fastened the latch.

Near the foot of her bed, her suitcase sat atop the luggage rack. She opened the closet door beside her and took off her blue sweater shawl. Exhaustion dropped on her from seemingly nowhere, and in sight of her bed, her tiredness kicked in. It'd been a long day.

A good day though, she thought and smiled, stripping off her dress. She hung both on hangers and shut the closet door. *A great day*, she corrected, and it had been.

With her eyes growing heavy, she moved to her suitcase and changed into her pajamas. By the door, she turned the light off again, and in the dark, shuffled back to her bed. She crawled under the covers and pulled them up to her chin. Tomorrow was a big day.

One of twenty, she thought as her eyes closed.

"Mary Joan, the mind-bogglin' Boggler."

She thought of Scarlett and her friends back home. She thought of the new friends she made that she'd see in the morning.

"See you at eight."

Eddie's grin flooded the forefront of her mind. Then Rose's smile. Their shared laughter. As she fell asleep, she dreamt of a trophy, too big for the display case back at the home, with her name on a placard across the bottom. She dreamt of her friends laughing, and hugging, and congratulating her as she made them proud.

"And our twentieth player who will be proceeding to the second round of the tournament tomorrow is..."

She dreamt of seeing the smiles on all her friend's faces when she returned from the competition that week, whether she won or not. She drifted off into the waves of dreams and her mind filled with warmth, and good memories, and hope as she sunk.

14

Michael sat behind the wheel of his car, driving. In the front passenger, Vince Kinneman accompanied him. His eyes burned holes into the streets around him. Neither of them spoke. He scoured everything with his eyes, prying, searching. Their headlights pierced the growing dusk of the night. His mind raced. His child was missing. His boy, his only son. Dylan Jones Grant. He was ten. God, he was only ten.

Father, don't forsake me. Please, God, don't forsake me, he thought as the face of his son ran clear as water over his eyes. Again and again, again and again. He saw their last trip together to Florida, visiting Lisa's parents in Tampa, spending days on the beach. The image of his son sitting in the sand, looking up at him, stained his retinas. His son's smile. His red swimsuit. His plastic shovel and printed pail. The worn image of a cartoon crab smiling from the side, *Visit Tampa!* running beneath it. He saw his son squinting up at him.

The thin skin of sweat that slicked his hair to his brow.

"Whatcha buildin' there, buddy?"

"A sandcastle!"

"Mind if I help?"

Dylan was missing. His son was gone.

"We've notified all patrol cars currently on duty. All our eyes are on the streets," the officer had told them, "We're doing everything we can."

Two hours had gone by since he last saw his boy. It had been two hours since he went out to play.

"I'm going to play with Kenny!" he remembered his son calling, as he ran past the office and out the front door.

"Okay. Just right out front?" he asked.

"Yeah!"

"Okay, have fun. Don't go too far," he said, and the front door closed. He never turned around from facing his computer. He only heard his voice, then looked through the front window to see the back of his son's head as he went to play in the cul-de-sac.

A missing child was what they classified his son as. A missing child, classified as at-risk, due to being 13 years of age or younger, outside of the zone of safety for his age, and absent in a way that was inconsistent with his established patterns of behavior, wherein the deviation could not be readily explained. Question after question.

"Was your son in the company of anyone else who could present an endangerment to his welfare?"

"Does he have any mental or behavioral disabilities?"

"Is he drug dependent? Does he take any prescription medication, with a dependency that could be considered potentially life-threatening?

"What's your son's height? Weight? Hair color? Eye color?"

"What was he wearing when you last saw him?"

"What color shoes? Socks? Pants? Shirt? Underwear?"

Michael answered every question to the best of his abilities, filled out all necessary paperwork, gave his statement, and provided the most recent pictures he had of Dylan. Several 8x10s of Dylan at the beach and with his grandparents, embraced in a hug. Videos of them all at the beach, laughing, playing.

An expanded investigation was initiated and the most recent photo of his son, along with all identifying features and information, were entered into the National Crime Information Center and the Missouri Uniform Law Enforcement System. Everything was explained to him by the officer, including what they were doing and why they were doing it, but everything blurred by. They searched his house and then the Kinneman's. People came and went, but nothing stuck. Nothing stayed with him. He only did as he was told. They asked when, where, and who all had last seen Dylan and Kenny. His lips answered for him regarding any overlooked or forgotten details that would explain their absence.

A perimeter was created and the officers on duty, as well as all friends and neighbors, began searching all adjacent streets. The first search zone, as explained to him by Officer Kelton, the supervisor assigned to their case, was how far their child could have traveled given his age and the timeframe. The area was a radius of five miles. It'd been less than an hour since his son went missing. Around 55 minutes, and continuously counting.

"The first 72 hours are the most crucial," he informed him. *"It's likely that we'll find him very quickly, but we need to start looking immediately."*

Back at home his wife waited with another policeman, one of the first responders, Officer Cary, in case their son came back.

"There's always the chance that your son finds his way back home. I'd suggest someone stay at the house, along with one of our officers, in case he comes back. Perhaps your wife would be best," Keltner offered, witnessing her fainting spell in the

Hall's front yard. Keltner had been the quickest to react, next to Michael, helping to grab and lower his wife before she could hit the ground. If they hadn't acted so quickly, she would have hit her head on the concrete drive.

From there, the other officers headed out, as did everyone in their search party, dividing into sweeps through their connecting neighborhoods. Surrounding areas, abandoned vehicles, and other places of concealment such as abandoned appliances, pools, wells, sheds, were all advised as areas to search. So, they all set out under specific instructions and began their separate searches.

Michael turned down Jefferson Avenue and the car's lights illuminated an empty street before them of abandoned housing. Sunken, sullen, soured houses grew around them, lining the road. To both sides, they stood like toadstools, crooked and gray. Dying grass grew over the sidewalks. Remnants of long-gone residents littered the lawns. Trash clogged sewer drains and caught in every available crack and crevice it could find. The road rotted and pitted, potholing, crumbling.

The car jittered over the asphalt and gravel flung from beneath their tires. Michael steered down the disintegrating road, searching all the houses. Each stared back at him with eyes like sockets, broken windows and doors torn off. Up ahead, on the right side of the road sat a white van with its tires on the curb. No other vehicles were parked in sight. Only rusted out shells, decaying in empty lots. The van still had all its tires. None were flat or popped. No windows were busted. It looked near new.

"Stop, Michael," Vince started to say but he had already started pressing the brake, slowing the car to a roll. On the ground by the van was a pile of torn fabric. Shredded clothes.

Michael shoved the gear in park, threw open his door, and stumbled from the car. He ran down the road and in the yellow of his headlights, dropped to his knees by the side of the van. To his left laid the cover of a manhole. Directly beside it, the perfect circle of a hole in the street. A black crater into pitch darkness. Michael grabbed at the pile of clothes. The tatters lifted in his hands. It was the remains of a yellow, long sleeve t-shirt. Beneath, the shredded remnants of dark blue jeans, socks, red converse, and inside, wood. Long bleached pieces of wood poked out from the tears, stark white against the colors.

These are Dylan's clothes. This is Dylan's shirt that he was wearing.

"Hey! Hey!" he heard Vince yell, and Michael looked behind him, then ahead to see Vince running out of the vehicle, then out of the reach of the headlights, to a figure ahead, staggering past the front of the van. The silhouette faced away from them, staggering down the street. His body swayed side to side.

"Hey! Stop!" Vince ran after the man and Michael looked down at the clothes in his hands.

Bones in them. There are bones in them, his mind spoke, but didn't process. *Not wood, but bones. There are bones in your son's clothes.*

"Stop!" Vince screamed as he grabbed the man. His hands grabbed fists of the man's coat and whipped him around. "Hey!" he screamed, and his voice cut off. As he turned the man around, Michael saw his face in the headlights. The man's jaw hung, slack, open. Where his eyes used to be were two holes. No tongue moved in the man's mouth, nor gums. Michael saw the white of the man's jawbone, but no pink. Only white bone. Where his cheeks should have been, decimated flesh hung in loose flaps. The man nodded forward. His weight fell upon Vince and his scream returned. As the man's dead weight fell forward, black liquid surged from his open mouth and spewed upon Vince.

"Jesus Christ!" Vince cried and fell backwards onto the street, the body falling atop him. Oil gushed from the corpse's mouth, covering Vince's face, crawling over his head, moving, squirming.

The liquid pulsated over his skin and his screams turned to inhuman shrieks as the wave blanketed him. Michael saw it moving. Thousands of crawling shells covered him. Glistening sequins. Writhing. Jittering. His open mouth filled, and his screams drowned to gargled rasps, wet gurgling.

Michael dropped the clothes in his hands and scrambled backwards. He watched as Vince's body seized upon the ground. His back arched and the horrible, retching noises seeped from his mouth. His hands stretched out. His limbs contorted. He could see no part of Vince. Only the outline of a human body, covered in scales, slick, shining, wet. Over his body, the scales moved like liquid.

The clothes fell to the ground, the bones in them clicking against one another. Michael staggered to his feet and ran to the car. His shoes clapped against the pavement. He threw himself inside the cab and slammed the gear in reverse as the black wave formed a rivulet and began to flow toward the vehicle. The headlights illuminated the spreading line, flowing from Vince's body. White bone surfaced through the covering.

Michael hit the gas and raced backwards down the avenue. At the start of the street, he twisted the wheel, punched the car into drive, and took off forward.

Those were your son's bones those were your son's

bones those were your son's bones, his mind repeated, but he couldn't listen.

"They ate him, Jesus Christ, they ate him, they ate him, they ate him…"

His lips bumbled of their own volition. Sweat poured from his every pore. His eyes glared at the road. His hands steered the wheel, and his mind took him home. At every turn, he twisted the wheel, sending his car screeching over the asphalt. On the main drag, at the intersection of Battlefield and Warner, a car zoomed by him, blasting through a red light. He took no heed. No other cars came or went. He ran through a red without stopping. Another red. Then, steered the car right. His wheels tore over the road. The engine roared and the frame shuddered. He skidded down the boulevard to his house, past neighbors, friends, home after home, until he reached his own. His brakes squealed as he burned to a stop in front of his drive. The gear cranked into park. The driver's door flew open. He burst from the car, the engine running behind him.

His feet slammed up the paved walkway to his front door. He threw the door open. It wasn't locked.

"There's always the chance that your son finds his way back home."

"Lisa!" Michael yelled, dashing into the house.

In the front office, the light was still on. No one was in the living room. He ran into the kitchen. "Lisa!"

The officer. Where was the officer?

"I'd suggest someone stay at the house, along with one of our officers, in case he comes back. Perhaps your wife would be best."

"Lisa!" he called and stopped dead at the entrance. His hand gripped the marble countertop. In the middle of the room, sprawled over the floor, were two piles of clothes, soaked in gore. A pair of jeans and a sweatshirt and a police uniform. Under the clothes, jagged edges distorted their shapes. Bones jutted through torn stitching. Blood soaked the tiled floor. The walls. The stove. Viscera sprayed the stainless-steel sink and refrigerator. Screaming skulls laid bleeding on the floor. Their jaws stretched open. Teeth scattered the ground. Cracks broke their craniums as if something had tried to push out from inside. Flesh and hair clotted on bone. Stripped hands reached out from sleeves. A putrefied smell rose from the bodies, each contorted in inhuman positions. His wife's ring circled a skeletal finger.

Michael gagged and a thin buzzing rose from the sink. He vomited on the floor. The sound grew louder. Incessant. Chittering. A thousand mouths chewing. A rainstick stuck in a paint shaker. A coiled rattlesnake. Cicadas. He leaned forward on his knees and his eyes tilted up as the sound grew deafening. From the sink, the noise squealed, and a glut of brackish water flowed over the lip, before covering the sink. Bugs surged from the pipes, crawling out the drain, and the din roared in the enclosed kitchen. Michael turned. His foot slipped in the spreading pool of blood. His sneaker squeaked. He slammed down onto his shoulder. The bone cracked against the tile and blood soaked into his pant leg, cold on his skin.

He clawed his way over the flooring, his feet kicking behind him. The tops of his shoes slid back and forth. His hands dug into the floor. The sound pierced his ears. The smell of garbage and decay, excrement and rot, filth, atrocity gorged his nostrils. He gagged and pushed himself out of the kitchen. Sharp pain bore into his leg. He ran back past the living room and out the front door. Behind him, the chittering followed him, trailing, tailing. The pain in his leg surged up his body. Jagged glass twisted back and forth in his calf. He slammed into his cab and shut the door behind him.

His hand jimmied the gear. His foot slammed on the gas. As his car took off, he saw the living river run from the front door of his house, down the walkway. Streams branched off and scuttled out of the cul-de-sac, following his car. Others swarmed toward sewer drain pipes and disappeared back under the ground. In the light from his front office, he saw glistening shells swarm up his walls and cover the windows. A living blanket blotted out the light.

His hand shot out and dug in his pant leg, clawing for the pain. His fingers tore into thin plastic. Blood ran down his leg. Something popped under his grip and the pain ceased. Michael lifted his fist and watched curded blood drip down his fingers. Pieces of thin, brown wings stuck under his nails. Spined legs smashed in his palm. Dark, spotted shell. Twisted antennae.

He wiped his hand on his pants and gripped the wheel. Tears streamed from his eyes. His teeth vice-gripped together. He rounded the corner and in his rearview mirror, lost sight of the horde.

"I'm going to play with Kenny!"

"What's your son's height? What was he wearing when you last saw him?"

"Just right out front?"

"Yeah!"

"Don't go too far."

Bones in them. Bones in their clothes. Bones, not wood. Bones.

"Does he have any mental or behavioral disabilities?"

"Do you think they went to Kenny's?"

"I don't know."

Those were your son's bones those were you son's bones those were your son's bones those were your son's bones.

He tore down Battlefield and blew through every stoplight. No cars swerved around him. The night sat dead and empty. Only the lights flickered, green, yellow, and red, to no one at all. At the highway, he turned onto the silent freeway and disappeared into the dark.

15

His stomach roused him from his sleep. When his eyes met the dash clock again, it read 8:09 p.m. He'd been driving for nearly three hours. The road morphed into thread that pulled him forward. His attention wavered. He hadn't been there. For three hours he drove, unaware, following the twists and turns of the winding road. The sun set, the sky darkened, his headlights came on, the road continued, and so had he. Behind the wheel, he slipped away and managed to escape from his thoughts for a while. A comfortable numbness, thoughtlessness, floating took over his mind and with it came relief. When his stomach growled, it was like waking up from a pleasant dream. His eyes registered the road, the time, and the darkness around.

He kept straight ahead. Another sign passed indicating the speed limit and he checked his cruise control, still set at 65. Half a tank of gas remained, by the indicator. His stomach gurgled again. He needed something to eat. He didn't want to stop. He wanted to keep going, but now that his reverie ended, his tiredness kicked in. His stomach ached, empty and bloated, and a sudden weight hung from his eyelids, threatening to pull them closed. He needed something to eat. Something to eat and a coffee, then he wanted to get back on the road. It didn't matter where. He just wanted to drive. Drive until he ran out of gas or came close to it. Tomorrow, he would think and decide. The only decision tonight was to not turn around.

So, you're going through with it?

"Shut up," he mumbled, and no one answered. Only the road continued. Darkened houses passed by, off the side of the road. Farmhouses.

Homesteads, he thought.

Fields and barns butted up to each one. Wraparound porches. Picket fences. Political signs. *Take America Back*. Tractors sat waiting in fields. Cattle hunkered down for the night. He passed through a small town without bothering to read its name. The speed limit signs lowered to 55 mph, then 45 mph, then 30 mph, and he rolled through a haphazard community, before exiting back up to 60 mph. Behind him, the same style houses, all darkened and hulking, shrank to pinpoints in his rearview mirror. There was no gas station. Only a scatter of homes. Lifeless houses. A ghost town.

The night yawned. He kept his eyes peeled for a gas station and watched for deer. In the sky, the moon punctuated the dark with a near perfect circle of off-white. No clouds roamed. Only the moon swam in the sea of blackness above the horizon.

Light faded around him. Matthew drove and the darkness swallowed him. Away from the city the land around absorbed all light. There was no pollution here. No orangish stain or tinge. Nothing dyed the skyline, other than the moon and stars. Out where he was, the dark was pure. His headlight abrased the shadow but couldn't cut it. The road lulled, his eyes drooped, and his car bore blindly on. His head leaned forward. The car drifted right and shuddered over the rumble strip.

BRRRRRRRRRRRRRRRRRRR.

His eyes shot open. He grabbed the wheel and jerked it back, swerving into the left lane. He pulled the car back. He needed to stop. For half an hour, he hadn't seen another car coming in the opposite lane. He flipped on his high beams. The brightness helped, but not by much. A sign flashed past for a gas station, but he didn't catch the mileage. It had to be close. He reached out and turned the radio up, then arched his back in his seat. His spine crackled. He twisted his neck to both sides. His whole body felt stiff. Tired.

"Okay. Okay."

A light bloomed in the distance. The neons of a pump alcove simmered. He slowed the car down as the station arrived on his right. His stomach growled again as he turned into the lot. No cars parked out front. None lingered by the pumps.

He pulled up to the storefront. There was no one in sight. He twisted his keys from the ignition and stepped out of his car. Silence, like a wall, greeted him. Nothing moved. He stepped one foot, then the other out of his car, and relief swept his legs as he came to a stand.

"Where the hell is everybody?" he muttered.

He closed his door behind him, and the sound echoed across the concrete lot. His eyes swept the station. Behind the front glass of the shop, there was no one inside. No one he could see at least. No customers, no cashier at the register, no sallow-faced kid mopping the floors. On the highway behind him, no cars traveled by. He stood, waiting, and watching, but nothing sounded. No cars came into sight. None traveled from the left or right. Only the quiet and the dark, continued, unabated. The lights of the alcove, hummed, on and on. He locked the car and walked up to the front doors. His fingers wrapped around the metal handle and pulled. Cool A/C flooded him, and he stepped inside.

In the storefront, silence pooled like water. His eyes searched the rows of racks. He walked to the fridges lining the back wall. There was no one. A wet floor sign stood sentry on dried tiles, but no store clerk. No mop, no bucket. No music played from the speakers. The lights buzzed and the fridges hummed, but no voices. He walked over to the racks of chips, granola bars, cookies, candy, jerky and grabbed a bar off the shelf. The heels of his dress shoes clacked over the floor. Everything was audible. Everything amplified. A chill crept down his spine like a cold hand. A pit formed in his gut that he wanted to shake. He paced to the coffee brewers and grabbed a cup from the dispenser. It felt as if eyes were watching him. He looked over his shoulder. Someone would come out. Surely the clerk was in the bathroom. Probably taking a dump or maybe rubbing one out.

Or maybe he's out back, taking a smoke break or smoking a doobie, or, or, or...what does it matter? It's probably nothing wrong. Something innocent.

But then where the hell were other customers? It wasn't that late.

But you are out in the boonies.

He didn't feel that he was that far removed, that far gone. Where were the other drivers on the road? He hadn't seen one for close to an hour.

Or had you? Was it really that long? Maybe you saw them but didn't see them. Maybe they passed right by without you even noticing.

Maybe, but it didn't feel that way. It didn't feel right. That was the problem. Here didn't feel right. It wasn't that there wasn't anybody present, or that he hadn't seen anybody, but that it didn't feel right. His gut felt wrong. The whole gas station felt wrong. Something in his stomach felt like something had happened.

He filled the insulated cup to the brim and watched the steam rise as he pulled out a lid and pressed it on top. His eyes darted over his shoulder again, but nothing changed. Nobody entered the picture. No employee jumped out from behind the counter. No customers came in the front. No one emerged from the bathroom. No sounds came from it of grunts or groans or running water or flushing toilets. He grabbed his coffee and protein bar, stepped over to the register, and set his purchases on the countertop.

"Hello?" he said, and the walls threw his voice back at him. "Hello?" he called, and his voice sounded foreign and unwelcomed.

He dug into wallet and took out a five and two ones. Enough for the coffee and bar, and whatever taxes on top. He pushed them over the counter, folding them under the register. Then he turned and walked away. *Click. Click. Click.* The noise circled his ears, too loud. He pushed through the front doors. Warm air ushered him outside, but the cold fingers never left his back. The deep sinking in his stomach.

No cars parked beside his own. The pumps sat barren, unattended, isolated, deserted. He followed the sidewalk to his car, set his coffee on the roof, and dug out his keys. His hand opened the door. He grabbed his coffee, placed it in the cupholder, then tucked inside. The door closed beside him and he hit the locks. Silence crowded him in the cab. He stuck his key in the ignition and twisted the engine to life. The motor roared, starting up in the lot. The radio came on again. Wonderful noise filled the gap. Although it was warm out, he twisted on the heat. Hot air rolled from the vents. On both his arms, gooseflesh stood out.

He tore into the protein bar and took a bite, and the sound of the cellophane wrapper crinkling eased his nerves more. His mouth salivated as he chewed, then swallowed, and within five bites, he demolished the bar. He took a sip of his coffee. It wasn't too hot. Not cool enough to chug, but enough to sip. As he raised the cup to his lips, his hands shook. He looked in his rear and side mirrors. Nothing. No cars.

Give me something, he thought. His wish remained ungranted. He sipped from his coffee as the engine idled and the balmy warmth flowed down to stomach, heating his core. Air like hot breath ran from the vents, heating the cab. Yet the chill remained. No cars came. His eyes never left the road behind him. The shaking in his hands subsided.

Time to get going, something spoke from inside. He didn't recognize the voice but didn't question it. His hand shifted the gear into reverse, and he backed out of his space. The car straightened then curved as he pulled out of the lot and back onto the highway. His taillights shrunk as he drove away before blinking out. As his car disappeared, a noise finally came from the gas station storefront. A low, subdued chittering sounded from drains in the floor. It rose through the pipes, quiet at first, but quickly built. As it rose to a roar, his car made it into the distance. By the time it echoed in the store, he was long gone.

16

Please, God, make it stop.

She was tired, oh God, so tired, and she just wanted to sleep, close her eyes for minute, rest. She just needed to rest. She just needed some sleep, but the crying didn't stop. She couldn't get him to stop.

From the kitchen, Charlie screamed and screamed and screamed and she had tried everything to get him to stop but nothing helped. He kept crying and crying and crying and crying. His cries merged into an endless scream, like an ongoing siren, with no end. A constant, blaring noise. An incessant tinnitus. Ringing. Ringing. Screaming. Screaming.

Rachel held her head in her hands and pressed her palms to her ears. The sound muffled but the scream bled through them, penetrated her flesh. Connor wasn't there. She didn't know where he was. It was past 8:00 p.m. and he should've been home. He'd been off for hours, now, but he hadn't come home.

But that's nothing out of the usual, her mother chided in her head. *I told you this would be your life. I told you this was how it would be. God, you were once so beautiful, Rachel,* the voice cried. And Charlie cried and screamed.

Her eyes closed, then snapped open like shutters.

I tried to warn you, Rachel. God, I tried to warn you that this was how it would be. I told you to get rid of it while there was still a change. I even offered to pay for the procedure. Now, look at you. Look at you! Where is he? Where is he Rachel?

"I don't know," she muttered, and tears swept her eyes.

You had everything you could've wanted. You had college lined up. You were a Varsity cheerleader. You were going to be a nurse, Rachel, and you threw it all away. He got you pregnant and took it all away because you let him. You threw everything away, Rachel. You threw away your future and he took it from you.

Sobs hitched from her chest and tears ran numbly down both cheeks. "But I love him, momma. I love Charlie and I love Connor."

But he doesn't love you, Rachel. He took everything from you! Look at where you are, and where is he? Look at where you and your baby live and where is he? I'll tell you where he is—he's out drinking and whoring with his buddies! He's fucking other women in sleazy hotel rooms while his friends watch. He's out fucking street trash, Rachel, while you and your baby starve!

Stop stop stop stop stop stop stop, she thought.

Charlie screamed in his crib and Rachel hit the sides of her head, again and again, again and again, again, and again, and again, and again. Stars bloomed in her vision, bright pops of white against the black backdrop of her closed eyes.

YOU HAD EVERYTHING LINED UP, RACHEL!

"Leave me alone, please, God, leave me alone."

EVERYTHING, RACHEL!

Charlie's screams turned to wails as she cried out.

"Leave me alone!"

Her hands turned to fists that slammed her temples until her head felt light. Her mother's voice ceased, and her ears rang. She opened her eyes, and her vision swam, in and out of gray. In the small trailer space, clothes littered the floor, the couch, the backs of every chair. Dirty dishes and trash covered all the counter space and tables. Must hung in the trailer like a thick cloud. Spit filled soda bottles and cans, lined the windowsills, floor; anywhere Connor sat. Charlie wailed, incessant. Rachel's vision steadied. The gray dissipated, but the ringing remained.

Crying crying crying crying. She stood up from her chair, mucus dripping from her nostrils, tears flowing down her face and sauntered to the crib to grab her baby.

This isn't what I wanted. I'm trying my best. I'm trying my best, momma. I'm trying my best.

No voice answered. Her feet stumbled beneath her. Something sharp pierced her barefoot. She took no notice. She felt warmth flow from the pad of her foot. Her hands hung limp by her sides.

"Charlie, honey..." she muttered, and her child screamed on and on, and on, and on and on.

She reached his crib and balanced herself on the railing. The screams turned to desperate howls and her ears felt as if they were going to bleed. Wails screeched through the trailer, then cut off in a wheeze. The sound of air hissing from a tire whistled from the crib. A thick gurgling. Then a rising sound. Wet smacking. Like a kid with a mouthful of sopping cereal. Crunching. Slurping. And a low chittering that began to rise, filling the gap in the noise. A growing rattling.

Rachel looked down into the crib. Her eyes cracked open, and Charlie wasn't there. There was only a hole in the crib. A black, charred crater where her baby should've been. An oily stain where her baby laid. Her breath caught in her throat and her eyes blinked. Again and again, again and again, but the image stayed. It warbled and jittered. Not a hole, but a mass. A moving pile.

From the bulk, four limbs extended, seizing helplessly. Two arms and two legs. Rachel watched as they jolted, as if hooked up to electricity. An arm slid down the side of the crib and flowed like grease between the rails. A pajamaed leg detached and the dark brown oil covering it, dispersed up the railing, and crawled toward her hands.

She felt nothing as the shells latched onto her skin and dug into the flesh, burrowing between her knuckles. Her eyes watched the slick beads of oil separate from her baby's leg, revealing only white bone beneath the tattered remains of his jammies and her mind stopped as the oil cut into her, covered her hands, and crawled up her arms.

YOU HAD EVERYTHING, RACHEL! A ghost voice called out, but she no longer recognized it as her mother.

Charlie, Charlie, Charlie, Charlie, Charlie, Charlie... her mind insisted, her eyes glued on the fleshless leg.

Charlie, honey. Charlie, baby... her mind cried, then thought no more.

17

His head sunk back into the cushion of the couch. He looked to his right at the tv remote. On the coffee table before him stood his bong. Beside it, his grinder, hash, and lighter. His head turned on his neck and his eyes swung forward to face the tv. Previews played across the screen, stuffing the space before the menu selection screen. His head turned back to face the remote, then his eyes. He grabbed the remote off the armrest and studied it, looking for the main menu button. The hit he'd taken was already kicking in and every motion felt slow and smooth, like moving in bathwater. He aimed the remote at the screen and hit the button. The trailer playing across the television stopped midway and the menu selection screen came up. He hit play, selected widescreen, and the DVD whirred inside the player, the screen going black before lighting up and rolling the film. The production companies faded up, one after the other, and finally, the movie played.

Stew set the remote back down and leaned back. The indica began to work at his muscles, rolling over them in waves. A dozen hand-held vibrating massagers kneaded his shoulders and arms. His whole body began to feel as though it were enclosed in a massage chair and his eyes glazed over the television screen as Owen Wilson and Vince Vaughn mediated a divorce settlement conference. His mind drifted as the movie played on. His thoughts were carried and he let himself float.

That was better. He felt better and the weight at his shoulders, piled up on his back, melted like ice, sloughed off him like snow, as the weed kicked in and his worries faded. Like an old photograph left out in the sun, they simply faded, and once again, he felt at peace, like everything was alright. It was hard to get that feeling and keep it, and more and more, Stew felt the only way to really do so was with a little help. There was simply too much to worry about. Too much to feel, that he didn't want to, or couldn't at least. He supposed what he had, if it had to be labeled, would be clinical depression, but he'd always hated pills. It had run in his family. Manic depression. Depression in general. Panic attacks. Severe stress disorders. His grandmother had been committed for a full nervous breakdown in her forties. But the only answer he'd ever been given by doctors was medication. Not that he'd gone more than a few times. Going in, he'd expected that answer—a simple one, a hand out, "Here, take this"—and when he'd gotten that answer exactly, he'd only gone one other time. When he got the same answer the second time, he quit altogether. Pills never made sense to him.

Symptoms may include: blurred vision, confusion and agitation, suicidal ideations, death.

It made no sense to take something which could cause exactly what it was supposed to be taken for to treat. So, for a long time, he just lived with it and got by the best he could. It wasn't until Marijuana was legalized, state-wide, that he gave it a shot. From a dispensary, he could ensure that the product he was getting was untainted. That had always been the one fear keeping him from indulging. Once he smoked for the first time, though, he understood that he'd found the answer to his ailments.

The thoughts never fully left. His overall depression, namely at the way things were and would always be, never departed, but the weed helped when he smoked it and left positive lasting effects, too. He noticed when he smoked that those good feelings never faded immediately. Usually, after smoking, they would linger and bleed into the next day, and could last him well enough until he got home to smoke again. And that was the greatest appeal to him. Because nothing he was intaking was synthetic, and because what he was smoking was something that people had been smoking for hundreds of years. Was it still smoking? Yes. And was smoking still not great for you? Yes. He understood that, but in his mind, the pros outweighed the cons, ten to one. At least, in his situation, and, he was sure, in many others as well. Those who lived with chronic pain, or others who thought like he did. Those who couldn't get over the hard facts of life: the facts that anyone in America, even those in the worst positions, were still far better off than those in other countries, starving, wasting away of a million named and unnamed diseases, those sold into sex trafficking, or slavery, or sweatshops, those working in coal and diamond mines, those children with missing digits and limbs, those children infested with pests, bugs, those who were living hosts, those whose suffering grew worse, day by day. And those who lived and breathed, every day, still feeling terrible, but feeling even worse, every day, for feeling bad, when they understood how blessed they were to even live and breathe and exist in the world and environment in which they lived—that which they were born into, none of their own accord, of their own decision, but merely by pure chance. Life was a dice game. And so, he smoked. Not because it answered anything, but because it made him feel better, and if he could achieve that, even temporarily, then what was the ultimate harm?

The fact that it didn't fix anything. But this thought floated far away from him as the weed kicked in and the feeling took over. He rode the feeling and watched the television and just coasted, because the larger questions were for another day, and for the time being, he could placate, ignore, and play blind. Because at that moment, to do anything else was too difficult. If that made him a weaker or more pathetic person for it, then that was just what he would have to accept for the time being. Because he couldn't deal with the bigger questions for the time being. For the time being, he simply wasn't prepared.

Outside the sliding glass window-door, the sun set behind the apartment buildings across the street. Several windows shone with soft yellow light. Others glowed with more exotic colors, tv lights and LEDs hooked up to change from blue, to purple, to green, to red. His eyes laxed and his vision mellowed, sliding from the window to the television, taking everything in slower, more articulately, noticing the finer aspects that would slip away under normal circumstances, unappreciated, unfelt.

Everything felt okay for that space in time. For that exact moment, he felt alright, and closed his eyes in gratitude, letting his head fall back and riding the wave, surfing, coasting, swimming in warmth. He didn't notice the low rising bubble of sound, gurgle from the bathroom drain and echo from the kitchen. By the time the sound rose to the room, he was too far gone to even register the sound. Stew sank beneath the high and fell fully asleep. He felt nothing as the pipes overflowed and the chittering screeched. Then, he was gone.

18

It'd been a long haul. In the front passenger, Marie slept with tiny Tim in her arms. The baby was fast asleep and had been for some time now, mercifully. In the back, Adrian and Bobby slept, too. Both their heads lolled off to the side, propped up against the seatbelt and the window. Everyone in the car slept peacefully as he drove. They were more than halfway home. It'd been Curt's idea to keep going. He knew he'd be the only one driving, and rightfully so, but it was his decision. If he got too tired, he knew Marie would offer to take over for him, but she'd done too much recently with the baby. She didn't need to drive. She needed to rest and do exactly as she was doing now. There was no need to stop.

It was only around 6:00 p.m. (5:47 p.m. to be exact) as he looked at the digital readout on the dash, though it actually really read 4:47 p.m.. Since last November, he hadn't changed the clock in the Expedition. It was just one of those things that he never got around to, so it'd read an hour behind for damn near five months now. In another three, it'd be right back where it needed to be, *so what the hell.* In three months, Tim would be sixteen months old. One and a quarter. He shook his head. Time flew, boy did it fly. Right out from under you if you didn't watch it. That had been the main instigator for their trip in the first place and he was glad that they took it. He was glad they got to see everyone and that they got to meet the newest edition to the Saddler Family. Timothy Redman Saddler.

It'd been Marie's parents that hadn't been able to make it down when Marie gave birth. It'd been hard on everybody. Since April of last year, neither of Marie's parents had been able to do much traveling due to declining health. Neither were ready for assisted living yet, but both had their fair share of problems. Namely, age catching up. Marie's father, Val, had struggled with bad sciatica for some time. He underwent spinal fusion surgery to alleviate the pain, only to immediately go in again for a revisional surgery when the bones didn't fuse properly. After that, it'd been a long recovery process, which, although Val claimed he felt better, Curt suspected that the surgery hadn't done much for him, other than crank his insurance and relocate the pain. Likewise, Marie's mother Colleen couldn't go anywhere without her oxygen concentrator, which made any long-distance traveling near impossible. As a result, when Marie had Timothy, neither parent had been able to travel down. They Facetimed them and sent videos over Messenger to keep them up to date, but in all that time—over a year total—they had never met their grandson in person. The trip was their first opportunity to hold him. That had been the main point of their weekend trip. Curt wanted his mother and father-in-law to see their grandson, and he knew it hurt Marie that they hadn't. It had been hard to schedule out with having a baby in the house again, and trying to find a weekend where they could go. As they reached the age where they could travel, they looked for a weekend. The first one that Curt came across when he had Monday off, they decided to make a weekend trip out of it, and drove up to Trenton to see them.

Time was too precious. That was one lesson Curt learned early in life, seeing that neither of his parents were still alive. He'd lost his father to a major coronary when he was sixteen and his mother the year after he and Marie married. For the blessing of having his mother be able to see some of their major milestones, he was forever grateful. He would never forget to thank God for the privilege of his mother seeing him and his wife join hands and being able to hold her first grandson in her arms at the moment Bobby was brought into the world at St. Luke's. Time was far too precious to waste.

Curt looked over at his wife in the passenger seat, their son curled up against her. Both of their eyes closed. He watched the rise and fall of his wife's chest, lifting and lowering their son. His eyes ran back to the dash and rolled over the fuel gauge. They needed to stop soon to fuel back up. There were only a little over five hours of travel left before they arrived back home. Estimated arrival time read 10:36 p.m. on his phone. Curt reckoned with stopping for gas and grabbing something quick for dinner for everyone at a drive-thru somewhere, that'd put them back in Sherman at around 11:30 p.m.. He was probably overestimating it, but even at that, it didn't sound too bad at all.

He grabbed his phone from the holder and darted his eyes between the road and the screen to add a stop at the nearest gas station. Beside and behind him, his family slept. A Flying J Travel Center showed as coming up in another ten miles and Curt added the pitstop. There'd be plenty of fuel, snacks, and coffee there, and he didn't think a big black cup of coffee sounded too bad to push him the rest of the way through their trip. He stuck the phone back in the holster and watched the maps update with the next programmed stop. The readout showed an estimated twelve-minute arrival time. With the volume down, Siri whispered that he would continue straight for the next 10 miles before taking Exit 72 onto I-44 BL, RT-266.

Yes, sir, Curt thought and smiled, looking ahead. He followed the blue line and drove right at the limit. He was blessed and there was no forgetting that. He looked over at his wife again, then in the rearview at his Bobby and Adrian. There was no forgetting it. *Yes, sir,* he thought and continued straight toward the Flying J.

19

Goddamn kids, Ian thought as he trudged down the hall. That's what it probably was. Probably some goddamn kids. It wouldn't surprise him. Now, that being said, it could have been some regular issue—backups happened, sometimes out of the blue—but even so, there was usually something that caused them in the long run. Something backing up pipes. Things that had been flushed that shouldn't have. So, it all circled back to the point: any way you looked at it, it was the goddamn kids. And the problem was, in his line of work, even when they grew up, the goddamn kids only grew up into goddamn adults. At least, physically, that was. But their minds never left that state. Their bodies grew, but they still acted like goddamn kids. Thoughtless, careless, uncourteous, and a pain in his goddamn ass.

"Ian, someone said that the rear toilet in the south women's restroom isn't flushing. They think it's clogged. Could you go check it out? I've already thrown up the tape," Vicki radioed him. Vicki the viper. The maintenance director of Battlefield Mall, and boy, was she a snake. Ian had learned to please her in her own special way.

To handle her like a viper, Ian thought and couldn't even muster a smile.

He'd learned quick, how to keep her pleased, which was, in short, doing what she said, without any questions. It was easier that way to placate the snake. As long as she felt respected and in total control, she never bit, never spit her venom. He'd only had to be yelled at by her once to know she could spew poison. The first time it happened, he almost quit. It'd been over a wet floor sign that he'd forgotten to put down. There'd been a spill that occurred—another goddamn kid, who'd spilled his triple gulp slushie all over the floor—and he'd had to mop the whole mess up, go back, drain his bucket two times, refill, then mop the floor in total, three times, to get the red and blue mess to come up from the tile. When setting out wet floor signs, he came out with two less than he needed, so he went to the back to grab some more, and wouldn't you know it, during the time that it took for him to go grab some more and get back to where the mopped tiles were—not to mention, three wet floor signs, already put down—someone slipped on one of the outlying tiles and ate it. He saw it right as he returned and his heart leapt up into his throat as he watched it happen. A middle-aged man Scooby-Doo'd it and fell flat on his ass. Ian dropped the signs and went immediately to help him. Luckily, the poor sap had been a helluva sport.

"Not a worry," he laughed as Ian helped him to his feet. "Please, don't worry, I'm fine. The only thing bruised is my ego." The man came to a stand, and gave Ian a pat on the back. "Truly, it's fine. My own fault for not looking. Thanks for helping me up."

The man went on his way and Ian set up the two remaining floor signs. He hadn't known that Vicki had apparently seen the entire incident, too, until later, when she called him into her office before clocking out that evening, after the mall had cleared out.

That evening, it felt like she had taken a switch to his ass, verbally. Not a word was mentioned regarding him helping the man up or his kindness during the incident. All that was beat upon, again and again and again for the better part of an hour, was how lucky they were that they weren't being sued.

"Do you understand how lucky we are, Ian? Do you?"

That evening, it hit 11:00 p.m. before he walked

out of the building. The mall closed at 9:00 p.m. and typically, he clocked out at 10:00 p.m. When he got to his car, quitting outright glowed in his head. If he did, it would fuck her over. She would have to scramble to find somebody else, and he could go get a job elsewhere, cleaning a church, or doing work for a venue. Instead, he went home, slept, got up the next day, went to work, and finished out the week. He kept his head down and avoided her as much as possible. From that point forward, when she asked him to do anything, he did it immediately and with one policy always at the forefront of his mind: CYA. Cover Your Ass.

Since that night, there hadn't been another berating, but he'd been careful since, and hadn't forgotten. Besides Vicki, the job was good. The pay was decent, as were the benefits and hours, and Ian figured it was easier to satisfy the snake than to find another job. At least for the time being.

His keys jangled from his belt loop as he trudged the carpeted main way toward the south side of the mall, past Aéropostale, Tilly's, Sunglass Hut, and Zales Jewelers. Carpet treaded to tile under his boots as he walked down the long open halls– if you could call them halls– to the South entrance of the building. The whole structure felt like a maze, and in a way, it sort-of was. Every shopping mall building was designed to keep customers in. Every aspect was built with the intention of keeping customers there as long as possible. That was why there were no windows, no view of the outside, and bright LED lights on all day long. Here, inside the building, you could spend eight hours and never know that the time went by, which is exactly what it was intended to do. That's why there were food courts inside every mall. So, you never had to leave. Working in a mall made it different.

As he turned down the maintenance corridor, with the metal double door fire exits, marking the end, he thought of how it affected him. The artificial lights did throw off your sense of time. It always felt queer going into work when it was light and leaving when it was dark. It gave an off-putting feeling, losing the light. It felt like hours were stolen from you, when you expected it to be different, coming out of the building.

The bathroom entrance came into view and sure enough, the tape was up. Not that Ian expected it not to be. If nothing else, Vicki was true to her word. She was a bitch, but she ran a tight ship. Ian stopped at the entrance and stuck his head in the divided entrance.

"Maintenance, is anyone in there?"

No one answered. He took his keys off his belt. Beside the bathroom was a supply closet. He keyed into the metal door and flipped the switch, illuminating the space. Inside, sat stacks of boxes, cleaning supplies, brooms, and the riding floor scrubber—and wouldn't he be damned if he didn't notice before, but the brand name of the floor scrubber was Viper itself. God, if the universe didn't have a sick sense of humor after all. In preparation, he grabbed the plain ol' bucket and mop, the heavy-duty plunger, and three wet floor signs. A spigot jutted from the brick wall of the closet. He positioned the rolling bucket under it and turned it on. Water spurted out. The bucket filled. He turned the spigot off and rolled the Rubbermaid bucket out into the hall before shutting the door again. The plunger and signs wriggled under his arm. The door latched, but he twisted the handle to be sure the lock caught.

Never can be too careful, he thought and turned back toward the bathroom.

"Maintenance, coming in," he hollered. His voice echoed back to him as he ducked under the tape. He stepped into the bathroom and looked around. No one was inside. He set the bucket and mop aside and came to a squat. No high heels or tennis shoes stood with underwear around the ankles. He was alone.

He grabbed the Rubbermaid and dragged it across the bathroom, the wheels juddering over every tile seam in the flooring. Water sloshed in the bucket. As he got closer, he looked at the ground. His hand reached out and pushed open the stall door. In prior years, he would've closed his eyes and prayed. Those days were long gone. There was no water on the floor. That was the first thing he noticed. The second was the bowl itself as the door swung open. The latch slid and clicked with a *thwink*. The level was higher than it should've been, but the inside was clean. Bless his lucky stars, clear water sat in the bowl. He already knew what he could've stumbled upon and sighed in relief of what it hadn't been.

Ian leaned the mop against the corner wall and set down the floor signs. He took the plunger from under his arm and stepped up to the toilet. This would be easier than he anticipated. Likely done in two minutes. He probably wouldn't even have to put up the floor signs. A smile worked its way to his face as he grabbed the plunger and placed it above the siphon jet. An easy plunge, then he could probably take fifteen for his break. In his locker, he'd been saving all day, a Krispy Kreme Cruller, promising himself that he'd wait until the end of the day.

Well, he thought, *the time has come, and I think I deserve it.* He damn well certainly did. *Just a quick clog fix, then fifteen minutes to myself.*

Ian pressed down on the plunger and gained suction against the bowl. He pumped his arms up and down as from the siphon, something started to loosen. A sour smell sifted up from the bowl. A strong, stale, rotting stench, sickly sweet, like turned yogurt and melting vegetables. He let one hand go of the plunger and coughed as the smell strengthened, invading the bathroom.

Christ, something must've died down there, he thought and the smile that was on his face fled as thoughts of the cleanup entered his mind and the work it'd take to get the damn smell alone out of the women's restroom. He thought of Vicki's voice, grabbed the plunger again and shoved down.

"I'll show that bitch," he growled.

A sound rose from the bowl as he heaved against the plunger at whatever backed up the pipe. A sound like maracas, or tearing paper, or buzzing bees.

Bees? What the hell is that? He thought as he pumped, but his arms kept heaving.

He coughed and a bubble of acid popped at the back of his mouth. His eyes watered and his mouth dried. He leaned forward on the plunger and the head bulged as something swelled into. The rubber distended as the smell choked him. His gorge rose. The suction between the plunger and the porcelain broke and what was clogging the toilet flooded out.

20

His shift ended at 8:00 p.m.. That was the one thing he tried to focus on as he sat with his head propped up on his hands and elbows on the counter, staring out. There were plenty of people, but none that stopped. Hundreds, maybe even thousands, flowed by each day. Out of that, about a dozen or so a day stopped in the store. Out of that, maybe two people actually bought something from him. His job was babysitting. Babysitting the store and watching over inventory so no one stole when the owner wasn't looking. Not that it would be hard. Inventory was loose, a fact he'd quickly learned upon getting the job. Everything was still ordered and checked in on paper and no one ever checked stock but him. That was his job. Checking in orders, counting inventory, reporting back, and watching the storefront.

And trying to sell sunglasses. Meeting his quota. Though, his quota was almost never met. People simply didn't buy sunglasses that often. At least, not ones as expensive as the ones they sold in the mall. Not with the advent of online shopping, they didn't. Austin lifted his phone off the glass. The clock on his lockscreen read 7:39 p.m. Behind the numbers and the date, a screensaver of Chris Farley in a plaid sport jacket, hugging David Spade smiled back at him.

Twenty more minutes, he thought, and then it was shut up the shutters, draw the curtains, throw down the sash. Twenty more minutes, and then he would dash away. *Dash away! Dash away all!*

He thumbed the screen of his phone and his face registered to unlock it. His home screen pulled up. Twenty minutes was nothing scrolling on Instagram couldn't take care of, so long as the camera in the corner couldn't precisely see him doing it. Adam clicked the icon and a message populated in the center of his screen.

Cellular Data is Turned Off. Turn on cellular data or use Wi-Fi to access data. Adam clicked on settings. No Service. The top left hand corner of his screen read the same. 82% battery. He clicked on Wi-Fi. No networks appeared.

"What the hell?" he muttered and his brow dropped. He thumbed down on the screen to refresh. Still, nothing changed. No networks arose. No Service. Nothing. From down the hall, a noise echoed. A shrill sound. Adam turned to see what it was. From the sound of it, it sounded like a scream. His phone set down on the counter and he stepped out from behind the counter. Surely, it wasn't that. He saw others stop in the main walkway and look out of various stores back toward the sound. Then another scream followed it and Adam saw the first of the mallgoers running, sprinting down the hall toward the north end of the mall.

21

"Okay. Just be back by eight. That's reasonable enough, isn't it, Sabrina?"

The conversation that they had that afternoon swirled her ears as she walked down the corridor, the time on her phone reading 7:38 p.m. Even if they left right now, she wouldn't make it home in time. She'd still be five minutes late, by the time they all piled back into her car and she dropped everyone off. When her mom gave her a time, that came with the mutual understanding that said time included the task of dropping everyone off that she picked up to go out with her.

"It's a weeknight and I think that I'm being more than generous with you, sister."

Ever since she'd turned sixteen and gotten her license, her mother had been a real pain. If she wasn't asking her to pick up groceries or delivering her brother Finley from school or soccer practice, it was, "Be back soon, Sabrina," "Don't take the highway, Sabrina," "Drive carefully, Sabrina,"

"Make sure you're not texting while driving," on and on.

She blew a strand of hair out of her face and turned toward H&M, down the hall. Patricia and Kelsie were still inside. She hadn't been able to find anything she wanted. Not that it mattered. She looked down at her phone. Ryan hadn't texted back. The last text she sent him was over twenty minutes ago. It didn't make sense. He asked her what she was up to, then she told him and asked him the same question back. They started talking about what movies were coming out and which ones they were both excited to see. He asked her if she would like to see one coming out sometime soon. She said yes and asked when, then... static. Nothing.

And it's probably nothing, she told herself. *You always get worked up like this when any boy expresses even the slightest tinge of interest in you.*

But that wasn't fair, because it wasn't true. She didn't get all worked up, she just got nervous. Like meeting someone for the first time, or interviewing for a job. That was nothing to be ashamed of, getting butterflies. Besides, this wasn't someone who just expressed interest. Ryan and her had been talking for a little while, on and off, and he seemed nice. He had a good family and ran varsity track (the 800-meter dash, specifically—Sabrina had gone with her girlfriends to Ryan's final meet last school year to watch him run, much to their chagrin and her, well, her indecisiveness over how she really felt about him and how he felt about her). He was on the honor roll. Everything about him seemed good.

Last school year, they had talked a little and then one day, he simply stopped texting her and she left it at that. She assumed he wasn't interested or that he had found something wrong in her that he didn't like, so he backed off. For a while, it hurt her inside, not knowing what had happened. She had hung out with him a few times after school, had gone to one of his track meets, and then in the Spring semester, their communication dried up. With new classes, their paths didn't cross as much and that was that. Then, when summer hit, he messaged her on Snapchat and said hello. Nothing formal and no explanation. Just a simple 'Hey' and that was all.

And that's all it took, her mind chided her. *A boy who showed interest in you for a while, then ghosted you completely, came back a little while later and said hello and now you're fawning over the opportunity for him to take you to the movies because he's cute.*

That wasn't true.

Oh, isn't it, Sabrina? If he was really a good guy, then why did he treat you like that and why is he so laissez-faire now?

He probably just got busy. We all get busy and it's hard to maintain connections.

Or maybe he's just looking for a quick hookup and he remembered how easy it seemed to get you, if he wanted to, back in fall semester.

I am not easy.

Time will tell though, won't it, Sabrina? Time will tell about both of you, won't it?

And the voice became not her own.

She looked down at her phone again, staring at her reflection in the black screen, the white lights above her. She thumbed the power button. Her lock screen popped up. Nothing there. No new messages. No notifications. In the top right hand corner, her battery life stood at about half. To the left, the phone read *No Service*.

Her eyes squinted. She raised the phone to her face, unlocked it, and went to her settings. No Service. No Wi-Fi.

"What?" she said. She scrolled down to refresh the networks. Nothing appeared. She swiped her pointer across the screen, again and again, and a scream cried out. Her hand froze and her head twisted on her neck to face down the hall. Beyond H&M, another scream arose and cut off. Others stopped and turned to gaze down the hallway. A flood of people appeared, bolting down the corridor, running toward her. Her body turned to cement. She couldn't move. Her eyes watched as people stumbled over each other, fell, trampled arms, legs, heads, women and children. The screams rose to a collective cry. A unified screech of terror echoed off the storefront windows and tiled flooring.

Sabrina watched people push and shove and run closer and closer to her. A man at the front of the crowd darted past her, toward the exit, and she saw another near the back fall. A sweeping, black carpet rolled forward and covered him. The man screamed, his arms reaching out, before his cries cut off in a gargle and his body overturned like a bug, completely enclosed in the dark fur flowing over the ground, spasming like a fish out of water, arms and legs contorting, seizing, juddering, then straightening, ceasing movement, and melting into the pulsing wave. The outline of his body disintegrated.

Sabrina got to her feet and fell back down again as her eyes widened, watching the slick, oiled, velvet tide roll down the hallway, closer to her. Another in the crowd fell, their feet coming out from beneath them. She watched as they flew face-first into the ground. Their head lifted and turned over their shoulder and teeth, like porcelain chips, fell from the bloodied mess of their mouth. Their eyes bulged as the flood swept over them.

Her legs worked beneath her and she forced herself to a stand, her eyes unable to pull away from the body. She watched it disappear beneath the black, break apart, and became nothing. Like a doll under a silk sheet, the limbs separated from the torso. The legs, the arms, the head detached. Under a thin veneer, the body was quartered, dismembered.

Sabrina turned and ran with the mob. Her phone fell from her grasp. People darted around her, pushing each other out of the way, running for the nearest exit. Her legs bolted beneath her. The light from the parking lot bled in from an alcove on her right. She twisted past decorative plants, trash cans, and benches and ran as fast as she could toward the door. A heavy-set woman crashed into the automatic door as it shambled open. The glass shattered and the metal frame bent before the door tore off its tracks and crashed onto the floor. Running feet trampled over her. Another man ran full speed and rammed his shoulder into the second set. The opposite door bent backwards with a squeal of metal and clattered inward. Spiderwebs shot across the glass. The man lost his balance and tumbled to his knees on the sidewalk outside. People pushed around him and the man rolled to his feet. He darted into the parking lot and Sabrina lost him in the crowd.

The heavyset woman on the ground stopped moving as Sabrina ran out. Her eyes caught only a glimpse of the lady. Shoe marks stamped her cheeks and forehead. Her mouth was bloodied. Both eyes blackened. Her face, beaten and bruised. Her eyes stared, open.

She's dead, she thought, as she ran over the pavement and onto the asphalt of the mall's parking lot. *She's dead.*

Keys, Sabrina. Keys.

Her hand dug in her pocket and fished them out. Screams continued around her, unending. Unending.

Get to your car, Sabrina. Don't stop moving. Don't stop running, her mother spoke and boiling tears ran down her cheeks.

Patricia and Kelsie were still inside.

GO SABRINA, GO! DON'T STOP!

She ran under the floodlights of the parking lot as her Vans beat against the pavement and her legs screamed and her nose and eyes ran as she sobbed. Her vision doubled, then trebled as she slammed into the side of her Chevy and pressed unlock on her fob again and again and again. The lights blinked and doors unlocked. She threw herself inside and jammed her key into the ignition. Her headlights came on and a boy, about her age, threw his hands up in front of his face, stopping, before collapsing onto the ground as the crowd behind him pushed over him and steamrolled his body. A car came from her right, peeling rubber out of the parking lot and Sabrina watched as the body behind the wheel, unrecognizable, ran over an older woman that was her mom's age, terror gripping her face. She watched the glasses the woman was wearing fly up in the air as the car crushed her body under the wheels.

The black tide flowed out from the exit she had taken and as she cranked the gear into drive, she watched the living flow pour into the parking lot. A mother carrying her child tripped over the lip of the sidewalk and the black liquid covered her. She disappeared. A lanky teenager wearing gym shorts and Nike Dunks fumbled with his keys at his car door and Sabrina watched the glittering droplets run up his legs, covering them, before swelling over his chest, arms, head. The keys sunk into the wave of ink and the body melted beneath.

Sabrina slammed her foot on the gas and her car lurched forward. Her tires squealed. The engine roared. She twisted the wheel in her hands and launched out of the parking lot. A shadow jumped into her headlights. Something crunched beneath her tires. Tears burned from her eyes. The car scraped over the speedbumps lining the turn-in for the shopping mall. Her teeth cracked against each other and her tongue caught between them as she jetted over the threshold. Blood sept between her gums and over her lips and she cried, careening onto Battlefield Road.

The speedometer read 40, 50, 60, 70, and held as she shot down the street, blazing past the red-lit intersection. A single car whipped by on the road beside her. In her rearview mirror, she saw cars with lights on, idle, unmoving. Others crashed into the building, smashed against brick. Misshapen lumps, heaps of clothes, tatters, remains, littered the parking lot. The sun fell.

Screams rang through her ears. Screaming screaming screaming screaming. She saw the old woman's glasses fly up in the air and her hand raise as the car pummeled over her, the wheels grinding over her body, crushing her. She saw the spatter on her windshield and looked through it. Her foot laid on the gas, unrelenting, and her car shot like a bullet through the night, past every light. Her hands drove for her and she steered onto the highway, unthinking of where she was going. The engine growled and her speed climbed. Her surroundings became a blur, the road, a continuous line.

Her mind stopped thinking, but her body drove. Sobs hitched from her chest and her thoughts froze. She didn't stop until she ran out of gas. By the time her foot left the pedal, she drove over 100 miles, alone.

22

Stanley took a hit of his vape and blew the smoke under the counter. His head leaned down. He sucked in and blew out a cloud of cotton candy-grape that fumed to his feet. The portable speaker behind him blared out music. He took his phone from his pocket and checked the song as a familiar guitar riff rang out.

"Fuck yeah," he said and took another hit. As a point in fact, he was glad the fuckin' speakers had finally given out in the joint. That way, at least he had an excuse to play his own music if Tharp ever bitched on him about it. That way, too, he didn't have to listen to the classic country shit that always ambled from the speakers before.

She took the house, she hurt my pride. She took my car and left my side. But she broke my heart and that's the hardest part.

Every one of those goddamn shit kicking diddies were exactly the same. To put it tamely, he wasn't fond of them or the culture they inspired or were inspired by. Which came first, the shit-kicking music or the shit-kickers?

Which came first, the chicken or the egg? He thought and smiled, sucking on the end of his mod.

Tharp always complained about everything he did, but never fired him, so the question remained to Stanley: why bitch in the first place? Why harp on him all the time for minor things that didn't make a lick of difference in the maintenance and operation of the storefront or pumps?

Why harp, Tharp? He smiled again.

Not that he needed this job anyways. It was easy enough and that was why he kept it, but if Tharp ever decided to up and out him, it would be no skin off his back. He'd get a job elsewhere and that would be that. Find the path of least resistance and tread water. Hang where you can, then get when the going's good. That was his mantra, his way of life, his code of honor. Why give a shit when no one else did?

The whole place was rundown, and such was a case in point for his argument. Even though he bitched, deep down inside, Tharp didn't give any more of a shit than he did. That was why he bitched so much and tried to keep Stanley in line. The logic was simple: if you don't give a shit, but things still need to be done, how do you solve such a conundrum?

Why, it's elementary, my dear Watson. You get the poor sap, the gullible schmuck to do it for you! You get what they call an employee, a subservient, an untainted chump.

Ah! Why didn't I see it before? By God, you're right, Sherlock!

Such was the case for the station he worked at. Shubert's. Shubert's Super Stop if you wanted to be formal, though Stanley never heard anyone, ever, refer to it by its full name. SSS. Too damn long. But that brought to mind the exact point that he never understood: why Tharp gave so much of a shit when it wasn't even his fuckin' store. He was a franchisee, as Stanley understood it, and as Stanley understood it, that meant he didn't own shit when it came down to it. The storefront wasn't his, and according to his contract—*You know my methods, Watson. There was no one of them which I did not apply to the inquiry*— which Stanley had looked up (*Shubert's Super Stop Franchisee Terms of Engagement*, a forty-seven-page pdf document, available online) in his free time, there was no ownership at all that Tharp was entitled to. Once he died, the store went back to corporate.

Article 1, Subsection E: A franchisee cannot pass ownership of given franchised location to any of their kin.

There was no entitlement to the family, nor

allocation of funds, if the franchisee were to become incapacitated and could no longer serve as the managing member—a funny word choice Stanley found in the contractual outline; very careful, clever wording. The gig was good for the person who got it, while they were able to handle it, but provided absolutely no contingencies for the franchisee, beyond the working period when said individual ran the station. As for 401k and retirement, there was virtually nothing. In essence, the deal was a crock of shit. Stanley figured Tharp would've been better off working for another company as a cashier. At least then, he could get better dental insurance.

Stanley laughed aloud and his voice sounded right at home with the roll of the drums and the blare of the guitar through the rechargeable speaker behind him. In all the time that he'd worked there, he'd never seen anyone from corporate visit their location anyways. Stanley was sure there were reports to write up and deliver and numbers to keep up and meetings that Tharp had, but beyond that, there was no supervision. The condition of the joint was proof enough of that. The speakers were out. Half the time, the toilet clogged in the bathroom. Above his head, approximately half the lights had dead bulbs that hadn't been replaced for months. The to-do list went on and kept growing every day. But the beautiful thing was, none of it was his problem. Nor would he make it.

Outside, a Corolla pulled up and a middle-aged man wearing slacks and a sour face stepped out before digging in his pocket for his wallet. Stanley figured in about another half an hour, he'd peruse the storefront's selections, perhaps grab a hotdog and some chips, and maybe help himself to an XL soda from the fountain, gratis, to tide himself over until he got off in the morning. There were no cameras in the joint that he was aware of, so there was nothing to worry about. So long as he kept his trash and threw it away out back or when he got home.

How'd you get so smaaaaatttt, Stanley?

Practice, man, practice, he thought and laughed again, when he first noticed the smell. His noise wrinkled and the loose smile plastering his face drooped and then fell as he sniffed and inhaled his first full breath of the stench. A thick cloud of stink, like ground mist, spilled over the tiled flooring of the store and rose to his nostrils. He looked around the store. His mind went to the bathroom. The smell thickened, emulsifying in the air. It smelled like putrid garbage. Rancid, ripe, rot. Spoiled meat.

Christ, that was all he needed tonight, for the

goddamn toilet to back up. He slipped his mod into his pocket and stepped around the counter. Nothing spilled over the floor. His eyes slipped to the door of the restroom, down the hall, in the corner. So far as he could see, nothing leaked out from under the door. No liquid. No overflowing toilet.

Don't count yourself so lucky, yet, he thought.

It could've been that the overflow hadn't reached the door quite yet. He stepped over the tile and paced toward the bathroom.

Just get ready for the worst, he thought as his hand reached out and paused, midair, before the metal push handle. Here, by the door, the smell was even worse and as he shoved the door open, he pressed his arm against his mouth, biting his bicep to push back the urge to throw up.

Christ, that's awf—

His thought cut off as the door swung wide and he saw the porcelain throne in the single-user bathroom. Except it wasn't a white porcelain latrine anymore. No. Not a single spot of white showed through. It wasn't the cracked and stained and usually piss covered pot that he had grown to abhor, scrubbing shit and piss and spit off of, wearing Rubbermaid gloves that reached up to his elbows, spraying the room with bleach and mopping it up as best he could. No. Nothing remained of his object of hatred that he recognized except the shape. The outline of the toilet. But it wasn't a toilet anymore. It was only the silhouette of one. A shadow. A negative imprint of what had once been there. A jittering cutout. Thousands of wet, shining shells covered the toilet, crawling, spreading out, spilling from the bowl, onto the ground, covering the seat, the tank, skittering up the wall. Stanley bit down into his arm, sucking in air, and his stomach twisted as the smell swarmed his nostrils, his mouth, sept down his throat and he vomited onto the floor. From the mass of the toilet, dozens of slick, shimmering jewels broke off and darted over the tile toward him.

Stanley let go of the door and tumbled backward against the wall. His lungs sucked in air and another breath full of the stench filled his mouth, splashing up the back of his throat. He heaved again, spewing his shoes and the wall. Spears dug into his feet and his ankles. His eyes swam down to his feet. Glittering oil droplets clung to his sneakers, slicing through them. Pain surged up his legs as the shells burrowed into him. He kicked his foot against the wall and felt three of them pop. His big toe crunched and fresh pain seized his foot. A sour stink, like turned yogurt, rotten cabbages rose from his sneaker. Thick curded slime, like wads of mucus, smeared his shoe. Blood trickled from the holes in his shoes where the bugs had eaten through.

Bugs. Bugs, his mind repeated. *Bugs.*

The skin of the top of his foot peered through his socks.

Bugs.

The fabric of his shoe and his sock had been torn. Sliced clean through. Chunks of shell clung to the running gunk. Under it, he saw white poking through red and yellow.

That's my bone, the thought came and held no weight in his mind.

Pain screamed in his left foot as another shimmering jewel cut through the sneaker, into his foot and dug between the webbing of his toes. He brought his right foot down on his left and the pain ceased immediately as the shell exploded in his shoe. Fetid white curds, like puss from an abscess, squirted out of the hole. His right foot throbbed.

He stumbled down the hall, toward the front doors of the store. Behind him, a high-pitched squeal rose in the air, like radio static, a tv turned to a station with no signal. His foot screamed with each step. Warmth surged over his toes, filling his shoe. More droplets flowed from the bathroom, squirming under the door, and skittered down the hallway.

Bugs. Bugs, his mind looped.

His hand felt for the door. He pulled the handle, crashing into the frame and flung himself outside as water sept from the station's bathroom.

Except it's not water. It's bugs. Bugs.

No, no, it wasn't possible. It wasn't possible.

The tide flooded out from under the door, crawled up the walls, pulsed toward him. Millions of brown-black shells darted over the tile, up the window, toward the ceiling. The lights in the refrigerators dimmed as the shells covered them. Endless bugs swarmed the gas station hall. Everything became an outline, covered in a moving skin.

This isn't possible.

How often have I said to you that when you have eliminated the impossible, whatever remains, however improbable, must be the truth?

As he darted into the parking lot, out onto the concrete, toward the pump alcove, the wave flushed out the front doors of the storefront, under the metal, between the cracks in the frame, and actually pushed it open. The door pulled back on its hinges as the bugs flowed up against the glass and found every crevice to squeeze out of.

"Jesus Christ, what is that?!" the man by the Corolla turned to him and Stanley crashed into the first of the pumps, running toward the man, toward his car.

"Get in! Get in!" he cried.

The man stood motionless, his eyes glued to the running oil slick, spreading toward them. His hand kept frozen to the pump, his eyes, wide, white saucers in his head.

"Jesus Christ," he muttered. "Jesus Christ."

He took the pump out from his car and Stanley dove against the car as the man began spraying the concrete around them with gasoline. Rich, choking fumes rose up around them and Stanley threw himself into the man's car, watching as, for a moment, the flow of gasoline halted the flow of bugs. The edge of the crawling tide stopped and withdrew from the gas and Stanley watched through the front windshield as the first row of bugs rose back on their hind legs and hissed. He forced his eyes away and glared toward the wheel of the car and the ignition. Keys. The man's keys were still in the ignition. Stanley grabbed them and cranked them as the man outside dug in his pocket.

His right hand held the gasoline nozzle steady, hosing the concrete around them, while his left brought out a small, metallic rectangle. The bugs crawled up the posts of the fuel island canopy and swarmed around the gasoline. The man flicked his wrist and thumbed the smooth, polished steel object and a flame appeared. Stanley jammed the gear into reverse and slammed his foot on the gas. The Corolla jetted backwards and the man threw the Zippo on the ground. Blue-orange flame ran across the pavement and licked upwards at the ceiling of the pump alcove. A horrible, piercing scream rose in the air and shells curled and fell from the posts. Fire twisted everywhere the gasoline flowed and the car burned over the concrete of the parking lot before launching over the curb and crashing into the station's pylon sign. Stanley's head slammed back and he felt something in his neck crack before all feeling went from his legs.

In the parking lot before him, the jittering, wet tide flowed toward the car, swarming around the flames of the alcove. The man at the pumps caught fire and Stanley watched as it ran up his leg, melting his slacks to his skin, before consuming him in a fireball. His outline dropped to its knees and fell over.

He'll never dry clean those pants again, Stanley thought, for no reason at all, and the thought came with perfect clarity, calm and unaffected.

The last thing he saw was the trail of fire licking at the leaking pump nozzle. Then everything turned to orange, and white-hot heat.

23

Paul stood before his window, his thumbs hooked in his beltloops, staring into the darkness before he realized what he was doing.

Let it be, he thought and made a motion to turn away that didn't play through. His body didn't follow. Either out of insubordination, or a desire to stay, somewhere along the line, the command from his brain didn't make it or was simply ignored.

Quit staring out the window like a blessed peeper. You look like L.B. Jefferies. You know how ridiculous what you're doing is? If you're so worried about it, why don't you just go down there? You waste more time off the clock worrying about the store than anything else. You might as well be down there.

He turned from the window and strode into the kitchen. He didn't want to worry about the storefront, but it was so blessed hard not to. Every candidate he hired never quite made him comfortable with leaving the store in their hands. Not that any of them were terrible—he didn't hire thugs or outlaws or criminals; no one with a record—but the kids nowadays were something else. He wondered where it all went wrong. Sure, there had always been bad apples, even from his time, but he swore that growing up, it seemed that there were just a better batch of kids that grew up into respectable adults. Paul missed the trust he used to be able to bestow in those around him. More and more recently, it seemed that the country was simply losing its values and those it instilled in the youth, in their children. None of the kids anymore seemed to care. But then again, neither did the adults.

If he had to pin it down to a certain time in which he noticed the shift, he'd have to say that COVID played a big part in acting as catalyst. Ever since the pandemic, societally, things seemed to have changed and Paul felt left behind. He didn't understand the culture anymore. The references, the anger, the aggression, the singularity in thought. He couldn't comprehend how everything had become so divided, people filled with so much hatred. You couldn't talk to anyone anymore about any politics or issues without being afraid of starting an argument or a fight. No one seemed ready to discuss anymore, or to set aside their differences and work together to come to a mutual conclusion. Everyone seemed out for number one.

Paul shook his head, waving away the thoughts. He sounded like an old man.

You are an old man, Paul, he corrected himself, and he supposed he was getting there. Fifty-seven was no picnic and he knew he was no spring chicken anymore. Maybe he was the one who was simply out of touch with the ways of the world, and he didn't understand it because it wasn't his anymore. The future belonged to the youth, but there had to be room to account for the experience and knowledge that age brought, too. It was all too much, sometimes, for a simple man like himself to think about. He just tried to do his best and kept to himself.

"Blessed are the meek," he said and the words came comforting to his ears as he walked into the kitchen to grab a snack to eat. A crunchy peanut butter and strawberry jelly sandwich sounded lovely with a tall glass of milk. Simple living was the key. You just did your best, for yourself and those around you, and didn't worry about things that you had no control over.

"Do your best and let God take care of the rest."

He pulled open the silverware drawer and grabbed a butterknife from inside. His hand shut the drawer and opened the cabinet. He took the peanut butter off the shelf, then turned toward the fridge. A loaf of Wonder bread sat twist-tied atop the counter. By it, a stack of paper plates.

Stanley was a good kid. Paul knew that. He was a good kid and an extremely intelligent kid, and although he knew that, he wished Stanley would too. The kid was a whiz, he just needed to understand his potential and realize it, rather than waste it away. He supposed that was why he hired him. In a way, he felt a fatherly sort of desire to support and train Stanley. Whether that was right or not, he didn't know, but his intentions were pure. Stanley didn't seem to come from an excellent home. Paul was aware of his parents and where he lived. Evergreen Park. Not the best place for an aspiring young man to grow up and learn good, solid values upon which he could build his life. Neither of his parents went to college, and as far as he understood, neither worked. Both, from what Paul had been able to ascertain from muttered grumblings and venting from Stanley, merely collected checks and blew them away each month.

Paul felt sorry for the kid and wanted to help him—that was why he hired him—but he was a hard nut to crack. It was hard to break through to him, and thus far, he couldn't tell if he'd made any progress or not. All he wanted to do, in the end, was show him the value of hard work and to inspire him to better things: a better life than the one he currently had. Maybe, though, it was out of his hands.

Do your best and let God take care of the rest, his thoughts echoed and he nodded his head as he spread peanut butter over the first slice of bread, before taking the jelly out of the fridge and spreading a thick layer over the second slice. He replaced the jelly in the fridge, pulled down a glass from the cabinet, and poured it full of milk.

It was sure easier to give advice than it was to take it. He smiled and stuck the milk back in the refrigerator. No one ever said it would be easy though. Life was a challenge, but that was what it was all about. Perseverance and faith. Do your best and let God take care of the rest, certainly. That was all anyone could do.

Paul shuffled to the kitchen table overlooking the valley, trees covering the rolling hills surrounding him, and the highway snaking through them below. The station, a vague dot of white by it, glowed, an illuminated island in the dark. He set his plate and glass on the table and lowered himself with a grunt into his wooden chair. There would be problems, there would be trials, there would be tribulations and there would be miles to go before he was called back home, but he trusted in the Lord and His plan. That was all he needed to know.

That's why it's called faith, he thought and took

the first bite of his sandwich, washing it down with a cool draw of milk. Nothing quite ever hit the spot like a PB&J sandwich and some milk for a late-night snack. Really, though, it wasn't that late at all. Paul threw his eyes over to the kitchen and read the oven clock. 7:57 p.m. shone back at him in segmented green.

Polishing off his sandwich, he thought that finishing off the evening by turning on the tube and watching another episode of Mike & Molly sounded wonderful. His sister had gotten him the full collection on DVD for his birthday, four months back, and he'd made it about halfway through the show, laughing the whole way. He loved Melissa McCarthy and every scene that she and Billy Gardell had together never failed to make him chuckle. They were such a sweet couple on the show. Great, truly great actors, both of them. As was Louis Mustillo as Vince. Boy. What a cast.

Paul smiled and drained the rest of his milk in his glass before grabbing his plate and coming to a stand. He'd rinse off his dishes, load them in the washer, and call it a night. No more thoughts or worries seemed necessary for the evening. What he really needed now was a good, hearty laugh, and he knew an episode of his favorite show would do it.

He scooted his chair back in with his hip when

the first glare of light flared from the valley. A bright, orange-white star erupted below him. A second passed, then the first explosion rang out, traveling up the hills, shuddering the windows in their frames. Paul dropped the glass in his hand, then the plate. Both fell to the ground and shattered against the ceramic flooring. He shuffled forward to the window, eyes glued to the station below, and watched as the second explosion erupted, and the pumps disappeared into uncontrolled flames. Flames licked the walls of the storefront. Another explosion rang out and the parking lot was consumed in fire.

Stanley...dear, God, Stanley, he thought and the glass juddered again in its frames as the shock waves flew over and up the hills and reached his house.

He turned and ran to the landline, screwed to the corner wall of the kitchen. His hand grabbed the receiver. His fingers dialed 911. He raised the phone to his ear and listened to silence. Nothing tolled out. No noise came from the receiver. He hung up and tried again. Nothing changed.

Outside, at the base of the hills, fire consumed the Shubert's Super Stop; the parking lot, the pumps, the storefront, and a single Toyota Corolla. The island of light burned from white to orange. Black smoke billowed to the sky. The fire raged and Paul stood in disbelief, trying the phone, again and again. Only silence on the line answered him. No calls came or went.

24

The feeling of weightlessness and gravity pulling down, accompanied by the ticking. The ticking of a clock, of a stopwatch, counting the whole way down, yet the ground never came, only the feeling of falling and falling and falling, to where she never saw the end. Mere seconds turned to minutes, and minutes became hours, and there was no end, until the end finally came and her eyes jolted open and a fresh sheen of perspiration slicked her skin, gluing the coverlet to her. The noise. The noise. Her mind reeled and her eyes blinked, dumb, in the darkness, as her vision adjusted. Where was she?

Where am I? her thoughts echoed and the voice inside her panicked, the voice of a child following behind their mother who suddenly looks up to see that they are missing. The voice of a caged animal, being led to slaughter. The voice of terror.

From the darkness arose the outline of her hotel room. The bureau, the couch, the TV in front of the bed, the single stuffed chair in the corner. Edith slept beside her, her outline rising and falling, ever so delicately, with each inhalation and exhalation of her breath. She didn't stir.

Rose's breath slowed in her chest and the muscles in her face relaxed, drooped in relief.

You're in your hotel room, her mind offered and the voice came calm and collected.

Yes, that's just where I am, she agreed.

The air conditioner unit rattled by the window, filling the room with cold air. Rose shivered. She needed to go pee. Her feet swept out of bed and into her slippers on the floor. Sherpa lining wrapped her toes in warmth. The room was so cold. She wondered what Edith had turned the thermostat to before she had gone to sleep. As soon as they got back to the hotel room that evening, Rose had brushed her teeth and got dressed for bed. By the time her head hit her pillow, she went out like a light. Edith had still been winding down in the restroom.

Rose shuffled across the room and looked over her shoulder at her roommate. She drifted somewhere deep in sleep. Her body didn't move a muscle, save for the rise and fall of the blankets as she breathed, but the movement was so slight, Rose couldn't see it from where she stood. She turned back to face the restroom and moved silently over the braided carpet flooring.

What time is it? she wondered, and her eyes turned back to face the small electric clock by her side of the bed, but she couldn't read it. Incoherent green glowed from the digital face, but formed no numbers she could read, only visual noise. Outside the window, though the sheer curtains and drapes were drawn, she could see that it was no longer daylight. Only soft, amber yellow creeped from behind the shades, the warm illumination of street lights. But the room remained cold, so cold.

Rose shivered and closed the door behind her as she slipped into the restroom and fumbled for the light. She guided the door the rest of the way shut. Her fingers discovered the switch and she flipped it on. Harsh white doused the tiled room. Her eyes slammed shut and her vision became a squint. Fighting against the pain, she forced them open and her pupils adjusted to the brightness. A shiver ran through her again as cool air from the vent above brushed down her back. Her nightgown stuck to her skin and under the airconditioning, her sweat slicked body jittered. She turned to the bathtub and twisted the faucet handle. Hot water steamed from the spigot and she pushed down the drain plug. The bath began to fill. Steam rose in the air, kissing her cheeks. Her bladder tickled her again and she turned toward the toilet. The rush of the bathwater filled the restroom with noise. She hoped she wouldn't wake Edith, but she doubted that she would. She just needed to heat up.

Rose looked up at the vent again, then climbed atop the toilet lid. Carefully, balancing herself against the wall, she flicked the switch, shutting the vent closed. She climbed back down and lifted the toilet lid. Then, she hitched up her gown and pulled down her undergarments. Her skin hissed as it touched the frigid seat. Her bladder released and warmth ran through her as she relieved herself. She pulled a strip of paper from the roll, wiped herself, and reached behind her to flick the handle. The toilet flushed and she wiggled her right foot out of her underwear. The band hung loose around her left ankle and she flicked it across the floor. Her hands grabbed the hem of her gown and pulled it up over her head. The silk fabric peeled from her and she tossed the nightdress atop her undergarments. She braced her arms on her knees and lifted herself from the seat. The water in the tub rose to the overflow drain.

Rose turned the faucet handle left and shut off the spout. She set herself down on the side of the tub and carefully swung one leg over, then the other. Her feet dipped into the water and her skin broke into gooseflesh. She lifted her leg back, withdrawing it slightly, then eased herself down into the tub, first her foot, then her ankle, then her calf. The warmth emanated up her body and she scooted herself to the edge of the tub. She closed her eyes and felt chills from the heat run up her back. They unfurled from the base of her spine, up her shoulder blades, to her head. Her eyes opened, half-lidded, and she lowered herself into the tub, slowly, the warm water rising to her thighs, then her navel, then her chest, just below her breasts. Warmth blossomed throughout her and the goosebumps across her skin became rigid bumps. She closed her eyes again and leaned her head back against the wall of the showertub. Steam rose to her face and filled her nostrils. Across from her, the bathroom mirror began to fog at the corners.

She let her hands float in the water beside her. All of her muscles relaxed. Her face drooped in relief and her waking mind drifted, slipping away like a piling beneath a rising tide. Waves lapped at conscious thought and she floated, semi-conscious, when sensation rose, dragging her from sleep. Sensation like a hook sunk into her and tugged her from her midsection. A barb pierced her, snagged her in the middle and reeled her back in from peace, up to the surface of consciousness, and she bolted up in the tub as the sensation dug, and pain erupted from inside of her and her eyes looked down. From between her legs, the water in the tub darkened. A crimson cloud diffused from her and the pain shot through her again and her mouth opened to scream, but her breath caught like a thorn in her throat and all that came out was a stifled cry, the scream of a mute. Tears bled from her eyes.

Her foot shot out as the pain bore inward. Scarlet water splashed from the tub, sloshing over the side and spilling onto the floor. Her spine curled forward and her body contorted into a sitting fetal position as the sensation lacerated through her. In her stomach, a single white, hot needle pressed upward, upward, digging deeper and deeper into her, and her eyes seized in their sockets as the plug jostled in the drain. Shocks of white lightning flashed through her vision and her head swam with growing splotches of gray. With every beat of her heart, they pulsed in front of her eyes, pounding in her head, overtaking her.

From beneath the drain cover, a single slick, brown ruby squeezed into the bathtub with her, before pain erupted in the arch of her foot. Then another squeezed through, and the drain came unplugged, and the sound of water gulping down the pipes filled the bathroom, echoing off the tiled floor and walls. Flowing, brown oil filled the tub in its place and Rose drowned beneath it. As pain became her only sensation, her mind left her, and she slipped away from consciousness again, forever.

A horrible chattering noise grew from a muted whisper to a screech, and in the room outside, Edith never stirred.

25

She felt warmth, the sun on her skin, and outside, the grass between her toes, cool, feeling wet, but not wet, no, dry, dry and cool, her feet ran beneath her and a laugh escaped her as she ran with her friends, her striped romper flowing around her, rustling back and forth. The one her mother and father warned her not to get too dirty, though she knew neither would be mad if she did, *She's only a child, Richard, after all, Yes, I know darling*, and her father's smile permeated, as bright and as warm as the sun above her, and the perfect blue skyline, an endless stretch decorated with unending clouds, tufts of white and she laughed and ran with her friends, the sounds of their screams. Screams of joy, of laughter, of play, filled her ears, as did her own, *Edith! Edith, come play! Come play, Edith! Faster! Faster!* and she ran until her legs felt as though they would give out, but she never tired, and the hills of play rambled on before her, encouraging her to run on, run on, run on. Then, she was alone and no one ran with her. She was moving no longer, but sitting, yes, sitting, by herself, in the lone square of grass that was her yard. The back of the house, where she played. The sun was still shining above her, the clouds, the sky, yellow, white, blue. Her legs were crossed and she was much younger, still in her romper dress, but a prior one, a smaller one, an older one. A circular shadow cast around her, her eyes shaded by the circumference of a Sunday hat. Her arms dawdled before her. Short, chubby limbs. She understood that she was again an infant again, fresh to the world, before the sharp pain erupted in her legs and a cry burst from her. Her mother's voice called from the kitchen, through the open backdoor and her father came running, sweeping her up off the ground and swatting at her legs, her voice warbling, sobbing, weeping, and dozens of tiny welts appearing on her calves and thighs as he held her and swept the fire ants off. Her father brushed away some of the pain as it throbbed in both of her legs. Her mouth knew no words to form, so the pain remained wordless, only a noise. A cry, a continued weeping that seeped from her and her mother. Her father checked her for more ants and then held her to him, his heart beating fast inside his chest, the vibration of his heart from inside his ribcage, echoing through, circling her ears. His breathing, his breath, his kisses upon her scalp, his soothing grasp, and the touch of her mother, all of them together, together again. Gone for over fifty years, but there again in that moment. Soon, she stopped crying and fell into the deep warmth of sleep. She fell into the sun, the warmth of the sun, an embryonic warmth, beautiful sleep, wonderful slumber, forgetting the pain, and as she dreamt, forgetting the memory forever as she slept. Her sleep became death as all unconscious thought escaped from her. Her sleep became forever as she was eaten away, as she bled, as she slipped away, away under crimson warmth, away as her breath left her, and the warmth became her as she was unborn.

26

The lake the lake the lake the lake and the sun shining off the surface of the water of the lake the lake the lake. Bright white light reflecting off a surface like glass. Perfect white. The lake the lake the light the white the walls. She was in a room, a perfect white room, illuminated in ways she didn't understand because she could see everything. Beyond the room, there was nothing, yet she could see no walls, only pure white. Pure, bright white, extending on for miles around her. To her left was white, to her right was endless white, beneath her feet, extending forever, above her head, a ceiling she couldn't see. Just white, endless white, but then from the endlessness, she saw movement. There were walls in the endless haze, there were walls, and the walls approached from the distance, closing the gap, as did the ceiling, lowering down toward her, slow, ever so slowly, yet steadily. The endless miles of white surrounding her shrunk to the size of a large room, then continued to draw inward, enclosing her, and the space became tighter as the ceiling and walls closed around her, a white box. A perfect coffin of white, of light, and the walls pressed against her. They pressed against her arms and legs, folding her in on herself. The walls were pressing her down, smothering her, and they pressed in, pressed in, and her breath wheezed in and out of her chest and her heart hammered and she shot up out of bed, throwing the covers aside. She shuffled to the bathroom in her nightgown, moving toward the sink, flipping the faucet on, splashing her face. Cold water doused her skin and feeling, real feeling, came back to it. The cold on her hands. The cold on her face. The drip of water. Real sensations. Her heart triphammered in her chest.

You're having a panic attack, she told herself, *you just have to wake up.*

Wake up, Mary Joan.

And she heard her mother's voice, soothing, consoling again. She closed her eyes, focused on the cold water splashing her face, and felt her mother's touch. Her mother's arms, wrapping around her, bringing her to her chest, holding her close. She felt her mother's breath on her neck, by her ears, and smelled her mother's hair. Her heart rate slowed.

It's only a dream, Mary Joan, her mother whispered and Mary Joan saw her smile.

She opened her eyes and looked at herself in the mirror. No longer a little girl, but an old woman, surpassing her mother in age, reaching a stage in life she never did. No. She was no longer a little girl. A sharp twinge of sadness filled her chest. Her breath came steadily and controlled, but tears threatened at the base of her eyes.

She looked at herself in the mirror and saw her mother, as she heard her whisper.

I love you, Mary Joan.

She turned from the bathroom and made her way back into the bedroom. At the edge of the bed, she stood and looked down at the covers, then turned to the luggage rack. She changed out of her pajamas and into a pair of slacks. From the folded clothes, she took out a shirt, pulled it over her head and made her way to the closet. Her sweater shawl came back on, her socks and her shoes, and she circled in the dark back to the nightstand. Atop sat her keycard and wallet. She grabbed both, tucked them in her pockets, and made her way out of the room.

The door clicked shut and locked behind her. Her feet shuffled over carpeted hallway. She arrived at the elevator, hit the down arrow, and waited for the doors. They slid open, she stepped in, her pointer pressed the circular *1* and the elevator descended.

Get some fresh air, honey, she heard George console, as clear as day.

The doors opened and she stepped into the lobby. The young man from before wasn't at the counter.

Danny...

Yes, Danny. Her hand stretched out. Cold metal filled her grasp. She pressed outside and felt the warm rush of air as she emerged from the building and the air-conditioned entrance. At the edge of the sidewalk, she turned left and walked, following the path with no plan in mind. A white haze of sleep still clung to her thoughts. The feeling of panic. A dark cloud of sadness.

Movement. Movement would help. She breathed in the air—fresh, warm summer air—like drinking tea. Each inhalation went down sweet, smooth on her palate, and eased the tightness in her chest. With each breath, the cloud abated. She slowly rose from the fog as her feet kept moving and the air flowed in and out of her. She felt as if she was in a dream that she couldn't wake from.

Somewhere in the distance, a siren wailed and tires screeched. Streetlights poured amber spotlights onto the road and dusk settled, the sun gone from the skyline. She stepped down the pavement, and her feet moved, one after the other, step after step. She walked, trying to force away the haze. Numbness swam in her head, but the cloud wouldn't leave.

I'll always be here, Mary Joan, George whispered. *Always. Always.*

The tears that threatened to overflow in the bathroom rose again to her eyes and spilled over her cheeks. Sadness bloomed into a cold, dark flower in her heart, shuddering down her back. Its petals unfurled, blossoming in her chest.

I do. She saw her husband at the Chapel, their families surrounding them, his lips pressed against hers, her mother and father crying from their pew.

Wake up, Mary Joan. It's only a dream...

Her gaze stayed straight as she walked, ceaseless, ahead.

"Mary Joan, the mind-bogglin' Boggler."

If that were so, why did sadness fill her now? Her thoughts ran over Scarlett and her friends back home, her new friends, Eddie and Rose, their smiles, the laughter they'd just shared. Good things had come into her life. Great things. Wonderful people. Her life was filled with beautiful people. She was blessed, so very blessed, yet the tears flowed down her cheeks. Just as she thought of how proud everyone would be back home if she were to win, she thought of herself alone, those she loved closest passing away, having no one to share her life with, her emotions, her love. She thought of her mother and father, the children she never had, her husband, all gone from her, and her alone. Alone and afraid. Alone and ready. Ready to leave, if this was it. If all that was left was a theatre of pain, and the only distractions were temporary ones. But that wasn't the case. Every day was a blessing. She knew that. Every day spent in good health was a blessing from the Lord, but understanding of that fact didn't help. Knowing God was good didn't make her pain disappear. It didn't help it or alleviate it. When the pain came, it simply sat. Often, there was nothing you could do. Time was the only healer. Time and laughter. Time and love. Time and light. Light and life. For, if light was the opposite of dark, and life, opposite death, then only focusing on the good could distract from the bad. The bad never went away, but shifting focus made it possible. Made life possible. Focusing on the good made life worth living. She knew that, but knowing didn't heal. It only helped point the right direction.

The Lord my God will enlighten my darkness.

God pointed in the right direction, but you had to follow—*Trust in the Lord will all your heart, and do not lean on your own understanding*—but it was such a hard road to follow and she didn't understand. Not in the end.

That's why it's called faith, Mary Joan, her mother

whispered, tenderly.

"See you at eight."

Because strait is the gate, and narrow is the way—

She didn't understand sometimes. She didn't know. But she had to trust. She had to trust that there was a plan. That God had some plan.

"Called in today and signed you up. You're all set little girl. You go make us proud."

Mary Joan walked down the sidewalk, forcing her steps, crying, blind.

—which leadeth unto life, and few there be that find it.

A warm breeze sputtered around her. Trash blew down the street, rattling into gutters. The sound of the city ran on the wind. Her feet moved and she focused on nothing at all. Tears flowed from her and she moved ahead, towards nothing, one foot after the other. She thought of everything and walked.

27

There was no real reason that he stopped, yet he did. In a split moment decision, he pulled over on the side of the road and picked the woman up. Then, she was in his truck and the two were driving, driving as far away from the place as they could, as quickly as they could. There was no logic in it, none at all, yet that was what he did. Then, there was nothing, nothing, nothing, nothing, nothing, nothing, nothing, nothing, nothing, nothing, nothing, nothing, nothing, nothing, nothing, nothing, nothing, nothing, nothing that he could remember. Only picking her up and then driving. Driving. Driving. Driving. Driving. Driving away and escaping. Driving away and surviving. Driving as the city behind them fell into chaos. He drove. He and the woman survived. He drove as the city behind them fell.

28

He didn't know how long he'd been driving when the low fuel light came on, but for miles there'd been nothing but darkness, extending darkness, as he drove and drove and drove. The single white light of the diner, neon, fluorescent, against the silk black backdrop of the night, shone like a beacon. Michael veered the car off the highway as he approached it and into the lot, kicking up gravel and dust. The red arrow sat on E. The car was done. The tank empty.

He threw open the door and looked around. Few cars sat in the lot. Sweat salted his skin. The keys sat in the ignition. The engine still ran. Michael turned toward the entrance to the diner. Above the front doors, read *PAM'S DINER*. Below the name read *"Good Food, Always Open"*. His eyes ran over the windows. A single patron ate at the counter. Behind the tinted glass, he watched a waitress bring coffee to another man sitting unaccompanied in one of the booths. He ran toward the front doors and flung himself inside.

"You've gotta help me."

Warm air greeted him on the sizzling smells of frying bacon, eggs, toast, pancakes, and coffee. Burgers. Meatloaf. Above his head, the lights buzzed.

From behind the counter, in the back, one of the chefs looked up, and his heavy brow lowered, watching the man who burst in. The waitress pouring the coffee turned to him from her table, as did the man whose coffee she was refilling. Both eyed him and waited in silence, waiting for him to make the next move.

Fresh sweat poured down Michael's face. Goosepimples rose on his back and arms. His breath hastened.

"Whatcha buildin' there, buddy?"
"A sandcastle!"
"Mind if I help?"

He clenched his eyes shut.

God, please, God, please, God, please.

"You've gotta..."

His throat clenched shut and the chef back in the kitchen, took off his apron and stepped up to the counter. Over by the table, the waitress pouring coffee took a step back. At the bar seating, the burly man who'd been chewing a Denver omelet, set his fork down and twisted on the stool seating to face him. One booted foot pressed on the ground, the other on the foot rail, ready to move.

"You've gotta help me, please…" he managed to whisper, but nothing more came out. Tears burst forth from his eyes and as he stumbled forward, a look of concern ran over the waitress's face. The chef behind the counter stepped forward to meet him.

"Look mister, we don't want any trouble in here. What's the ma—" he started to say, but that was as far as he got before a sound ripped out from the restroom. A scream tore through the diner, splitting the air. The noise shattered the silence and all eyes turned toward the door. None watched Michael as the sound tore out again, and then the door flew open, and what was inside came out.

29

It'd been a quiet shift that day, one fact, for which Dorothy was glad. There'd been too much on her mind lately. The kids, the car. Everything all at once. Usually, it wasn't until the end of the year that things came to a boil, but it all seemed to now. She felt like she didn't have enough time, not enough hours in a day. There was an oil leak in the Toyota that she needed to get fixed. The kids needed new clothes and school supplies coming up with their new semester. Money always seemed so thin. So, so thin. That was why she was working tonight, taking another double shift to help cover the costs that the Toyota would surely bring. Andy was pulling an overnight shift later that week. They were doing their best, but it hurt when your best didn't always feel like enough.

"We'll get it nipped Dory," Andy grabbed her and held her close as she was leaving. He was staying home, catching up on some sleep, before going in again at 1:00 that morning. "Nothing in life comes easy," he said and wrapped his arms around her, interlocking his hands at the base of her back, right above her butt. He pulled her to him so their hips touched. "I love you, honey," he pulled her eyes toward his, then leaned forward, resting his forehead against hers.

She said she loved him too, and they kissed before she left for the diner. Andy groggily turned back toward their bedroom, Phillip and Scott both asleep in their beds. Scott was old enough to take care of his little brother when 6:00 a.m. came if she wasn't home yet. He knew how to get him and his brother ready for school and where the bus would pick them up. They were such good boys. Phillip's eighth birthday was already near and Scott would be fourteen next Fall. God, how time flew by. You blinked your eyes and–

Dorothy turned toward the back shelving, grabbed a pack of coffee grounds in their plastic-foil pouch, and a fresh filter for the machine. She didn't think that anyone knew true love until they had children. It wasn't revealed until you had a child of your own and looked into their eyes. From that point, you knew that you would do absolutely anything for them.

She walked to the coffee maker, popped open the top, pressed the filter down in the basket, and tore open the foil-pouch of grounds before pouring it out. The lid clapped down, she thumbed the *Brew Now* option and waited until she heard the telltale gurgling of hot water hissing through the machine.

Out front, there were practically no customers save for Bernie, sitting in the corner booth, nursing his insobriety with another cup of coffee. The one she'd poured for him sat steaming on the table before him, his face inches above it. When she last left him, he sat soaking up the heat, his eyes bounding slowly up and down, along with his head, bobbing like a ship on the water. If there was a position to be filled for town drunk, Bernie would be it, but he was never a nuisance. He simply swilled, came in, ate, fell asleep (more often than not, until close), then left when they roused him. He always paid, never caused any commotion. Carey, the owner, hated the fact that he chose the diner to rest in after carousing– his favorite word to use when talking about Bernie, carousing: "I don't see why he can't go to the Denny's up the road after ca-*roos*-ing all night, drinking. He's gonna drink himself to death, I can tell you that much and I don't want him in my restaurant when he finally bites the big one, and seizes on the floor"– but Dorothy never minded. She felt sorry for him. Sorry that whatever he was looking for, he kept trying to find at the bottom of each bottle.

Besides Bernie, only two other patrons occupied

the front: a heavier-set, muscle-bound gentleman who reminded Dorothy of a cross between Ken Foree and Fred Williamson, and another man, quiet and reserved when she served him, long, lanky, and dressed in gray sweats. Ken Williamson sat at the bar and was currently chewing on the Denver omelet that Brett, *Pam's Diner's* own head chef ("Whatever the hell that's worth," Brett always jested), made for him. Sweatpants, in contrast, had left the glass of milk and blueberry muffin he ordered, unattended, at his table while he went to use the restroom.

Dorothy made her way back to the front, weaving past the grills to the bar seating and register. She grabbed a handful of straws on her way and tucked them into her apron, along with four more rolls of fresh silverware. By the grills, Brett leaned against the wall, a paperback novel folded in half between the thick fingers of his right hand. He raised his eyebrows at her as she passed, then darted his eyes over the front seating, checking on Bernie and Mr. Muscle-Bound before diving nose-first back into his book.

"Still doing alright?" she asked Denver Omelet as she swept by him, before settling at the register.

"Sure am, hun. Thank ya," he said. His face lifted, offered a closed-lip smile, and lowered, returning to his food.

There wasn't much to do then, beyond wait. She pulled her phone out of her pocket and slid it atop the counter, behind the register, out of view of the customers. The front read 12:39 a.m. Andy would've been off to work by now, then. She flicked her thumb up to unlock her phone and opened her messages when she saw the top left corner of her screen. No service. Her expression faltered and a frown formed.

"You've gotta be kidding me.."

"I'm sorry?" Denver Omelet looked at her and she jumped. His voice, even low, broke the air like a hammer. A nervous titter escaped her.

"Nothing. I'm sorry. Just don't have any damn service on this thing," she held her phone up and gave a courteous grin before tucking it back in her pocket.

Denver nodded and returned the smile. "It's alright," he answered.

In his booth, Bernie spoke up. "Say Dorothy, could I get another cup?" he asked and she saw that he'd drained the one she left him with.

"Sure thing. One second, Bernie."

She curved past the fryers, back toward the Bunn and grabbed the full pot out from underneath it. Water trickled steadily through the machine, filling the second decanter to the right. Brett noted her again as she passed by with the coffee. She wove toward Bernie with the skill and grace only mothers ever attain and tilted the pot to fill his cup to the brim without spilling a drop.

"Thank you, Dorothy," Bernie looked up at her, his head propped up on his arm. Deep, dark circles like leather baggage hung under his eyes. His complexion looked pale.

Too pale, Bernie, the mother in her spoke. *Too pale.*

"My pleasu–" she began, when she heard the squeal of rubber. Past the window, behind him, a car twisted off the highway and into the parking lot. Dorothy watched the vehicle swerve from the blacktop onto their drive. Gravel and dust kicked up in a plume behind him. For a split second, she thought the driver of the vehicle wasn't going to stop, but crash into the building, boring past the front doors before smashing through the counter and into the fryers. The car did stop, however, and a man emerged from the driver's side. As he ran inside, Dorothy's eyes stayed with the vehicle. The man left the engine running, the keys inside, the doors unlocked. Her attention twisted to the front door. It opened and as the man stepped inside, all eyes turned to him.

Denver at the counter twisted on his stool. From the back kitchen, Brett stepped forward. From the booth, both her and Bernie watched the man.

"You've gotta help me," he said.

His eyes darted about the diner, looking at everything, but taking in nothing. Both eyes glazed over, constantly moving. Sweat poured down his face. Fear shook the man's body. By his sides, his hands shook. He clenched his eyes shut and looked to struggle against breaking down into heaving, shuddering sobs, before wrestling composure and opening his eyes again. His breath sputtered out of him.

"You've gotta…"

By his sides, his hands now clenched into fists and his eyes clamped shut again, his face reddening to a maddening shade of maroon. The skin of his hands turned to white as his nails dug into his palms.

Dorothy took a step back and Brett stepped out from the kitchen, removing his apron and hanging it on the hook at the entrance to the kitchen. At the bar, Denver set a booted-foot on the ground, ready to pounce.

"You've gotta help me, please…" the man exhaled and his words came out a whisper, barely audible in the dead silence of the diner. Tears ran from the man's eyes and his face crumpled, reddening, warping in pain.

Concern twisted her expression. This man wasn't on anything. She'd seen men on drugs, on alcohol, out of themselves, and this wasn't it. Something was wrong. Terribly wrong. She took a step forward. Brett stopped her by stepping forward to meet the man as he stood shaking, in the middle of the restaurant.

"Look mister, we don't want any trouble in here. What's the ma—" he started to say, and then a horrible sound ripped out from the restroom. The sound of nightmares. The manifestation of what she knew to be true. Her gut feeling that something was wrong– horribly, terribly, utterly wrong. every eye in the restaurant, including her own, turned toward the doors. None watched the man as the scream shot like a bullet, exploding the quiet that hung in the diner. Then the same horrible, deafening scream tore out again. The bathroom door flung open and the nightmare emerged.

30

A gargling mass, the sound of drowning. A wet, slushing heap crashed forward onto the tile. The door slammed open against the wall. Its metal knob broke off and skittered over the floor. Inside the bathroom, everything crawled. A thick, moving carpet covered every surface. All was an outline. Michael saw. There was nothing inside. No stalls. No sink. No urinal. No flooring. Just a singular moving layer. It was as if the entire inside of the room had been coated in fur. Only it wasn't fur. The bathroom breathed on its own and what covered the inside flowed out. Shining stones, shells, leaves, crawled from the bathroom into the restaurant. Endless gems, oil drops, sludge. The rippling mass dove forward and collapsed. Arms reached out and as they crashed against the flooring, beads dropped free and dashed over the tile toward the dining area. The smell of putrefaction rushed into the diner and an ear-splitting screech roared the air. A horrible chittering, ringing, screaming. The screams of a man–*there's a man under there, there's a man under there*– morphed into the screams of the living tissue, and the walls of the bathroom flooded out, became a torrent, and crawled into the diner.

Michael turned and ran as the stench filled his nostrils, grabbed his gorge, twisted it, pulled it up his throat. Hot acid bubbles popped in the back of his mouth. Vomit spilled over his lips as he pushed past the man who had come up from the kitchen. The man didn't move, only watched, frozen in disbelief, as the wave flowed toward him. The tide flowed up the boot of the man at the bar and Michael heard his screams as he pushed into the back, past the fryers, and searched for the back door– an escape, a way out. The man's screams reached an impossible pitch before snuffing out. Then came the screams of another man, and the howls of another, before the wails of the waitress slit the air. Michael turned and saw the wave streaming toward him. Millions of bugs skittered toward him. He dashed toward the walk-in freezer and grabbed at the handle. He tore the door open and slammed it behind him. The shrill screech of the wave bore through the metal barrier.

Please, God, make it stop, make it stop, make it stop.

He pushed himself against the back wall, as far as he could from the door itself, and watched as a single jewel pushed between the seal of the door and the frame and darted toward him. Michael slammed his foot down on the shell and white, putrid pus erupted in a crunch from under his shoe. The screeches outside the door wailed and he slammed his hands against the sides of his head, covering his ears.

"Michael, it's about time for dinner."

"Would you mind telling Dylan to come inside and wash up? We'll probably need to call Kenny's parents too, to let them know where he'll be if he wants to stay the night."

"The boys ready, Michael?"

"I don't know. Didn't see them out there."

"Do you think they went to Kenny's?"

Those were your son's bones those were your son's bones those were your son's bones.

"Just right out front?"

"Yeah!"

"Don't go too far."

Michael pressed his palms against his ears, clenched his eyes shut, and clamped his jaw. Every tendon in his neck stood on end. His head pounded as stars exploded on the black of his vision. He opened his mouth and his scream became one with the never-ending shriek outside the door.

31

The diner brought his attention back and reeled it from the darkness to reality. It was the only light he'd seen since the gas station. His tank was nearly empty and his stomach growled again. In the cupholder, his empty coffee cup and the wrapper to his long-gone protein bar laid out wrinkled. The damn things never stayed in a ball when you crumpled them up. He needed fuel for both himself and his vehicle. Up until the lights of the diner, he'd thought of nothing. Songs had come and gone on the radio and he'd floated the musical wave as he drove. Nothing interrupted him, nor his drive. Endless country stretched on, pitch dark, perfect black. Ink surroundings and silhouettes of murk stained the scenery. His mind wandered and for the first time in a long time, he felt much better than when he first left. A weight lifted from his shoulders. There was power if he wanted it. Power to change. Power to say no. Power to get up, leave, and be done. And as he thought of these things, he felt there was room to change.

If you don't like your future—if you don't like where you see it's headed—then change it.

So, he would.

So, you're actually going to?

The answer was yes, of course, yes.

If you knew you were going to die tomorrow, would you still be leading the same life you're leading now?

Part of that question was ridiculous if you took it at that value. Throwing hedonism aside, the question bore weight and boiled down to a more important one: if you died tomorrow, would you be happy? Would you be satisfied with how you used your time or would you regret it?

Regret. Regret. Regret. Risk and regret. Those were the key words. For without some form of risk, would there not invariably be regret? If you always sat on the sidelines and never did anything risky, never did anything some might consider stupid because your heart and mind and soul told you that it was the right decision, because deep down you knew something had to change, would you not sorrow when the moment had passed? If you always took the safest path, if you never took the leap of faith, when you arrived at your deathbed, how much would your heart pang with the opportunities you were never afforded— never afforded because you never grasped them?

There was a decision he had arrived at, ultimately, and as the lights of the diner grew on the horizon, first from a pinpoint, then to a radiating island, he knew what it was. He was going to quit his job and find something new. He didn't know what, but that didn't matter. What mattered was the first step and what mattered was the direction that first step was in.

You've still got plenty of road to decide what comes after the first step, his mind spoke. For once, in the entirety of his trip, he agreed completely.

Yes, there was still plenty of road left. Plenty of road left and plenty of time. He wouldn't be going into work tomorrow and maybe not the next day either, but he'd be working on his own, figuring out just what he wanted and where he wanted to go. There was plenty of road left.

Matthew eased the speed of his vehicle down as the diner arrived and he pulled into the left lane. He came to a stop at the turnoff for the restaurant, Farm Rd 172. He checked both ways then pulled across the opposite two lanes of highway drive. His wheels rolled smoothly over asphalt to a crunch over gravel as he pulled into the parking lot. Atop the joint, a sign in simmering crimson buzzed *PAM'S DINER*. Beneath, in cursive script, *"Good Food, Always Open"*. Several trucks lined the lot.

A red Ford, two Toyotas, and a Mercury. Parked helter skelter up front, a single car sat with its lights still on. Lines in the gravel followed the vehicle from where it had skidded in.

Must've had to piss real bad, he thought, numbly, then found himself smiling at the thought.

The engine on the car wasn't running. Matthew pulled beside the red Ford closest to the road and parked. He twisted his lights off and pulled the keys from the ignition. The engine died and silence filled the cab. Pure, utter quiet, unadulterated by anything at all. His eyes turned toward the front windows of the diner. White, LED lights spilled out through the glass, but he couldn't see anyone inside. No profiles sat in the booths. No one at the bar. No waitresses bussed tables or mosied around the front.

Shit, he thought, *I hope they're still open*, and a laugh wheezed out of him as his eyes read the italicized descriptor again. *"Good Food, Always Open"*

"Let's hope you're not shittin," he said and his voice felt stuffy in the car. On the dash, he checked his mileage again, before unbuckling. 25 miles until empty. He needed to refill the car soon. Real soon. He made a mental note to search maps for the nearest gas station when he got back.

He pushed open his door and stepped into the

night. His hand threw the door closed behind him, hit the fob, and locked the vehicle. Both feet crunched over the gravel and the sound reminded him of the gas station from before. *Click. Click. Click.* Only now, *Crunch. Crunch. Crunch.* A chill like ice water spilled down his back, raising his skin in bumps despite the temperature.

Put it out of your head. It was nothing back there. Did anything happen?

No. Nothing had, but still...

But still, nothing. You're tired. You're hungry. Let's get something to eat and focus on what's important.

His feet paced over the rock and his eyes watched the windows as he approached the doors.

Nobody's here either, he thought as his throat tightened, making each breath feel like sucking air through a straw.

No response returned to him immediately. *Maybe there are only a few people working and they're all in the back.*

Doing what?

I don't know, his mind answered plainly.

His feet carried him forward and his hand grasped the handle. He couldn't see anyone inside.

Something's not right, he thought but no voice returned. His body moved and fear rose in him like a tide, boiling, seething. His heart raced and every beat slammed in his ears, beating his temples.

Yet he never stopped moving. His limbs acted of their own control, as if a marionette, and he watched. He watched his arm pull the door toward him and then his legs step inside, and as his eyes crawled down to his feet, crossing the threshold and stepping into the diner, he saw the flooring, the tiled flooring, and his mouth opened to yell to scream to shout but nothing came out. A small choking noise clicked in the back of his throat.

It's time to wake up, now, Matthew, his mind thought and his eyes blinked, but the vision remained.

His nose filled with horror. His eyes swept over the checked-tile floor of the diner. Blood covered everything. Thick, dark fluids sept over the black and white squares and bodies littered the floor. Outstretched corpses. Desecrated bodies. Mutilated remains. Near the booths, on the floor, two tangled in one another, their sexes unrecognizable. Shreds of hair and clothing twisted about them, matted in tissue, plastered to skeleton. Eviscerated organs roped the legs of the booth. Near the bar seating, a shattered tibia jutted from a steel-toed boot. In front of the bathroom, the door broken on its hinges, a skeleton prostrated, stripped entirely of flesh.

The bones are pink, not white, his mind thought dumbly as his eyes bulged.

Behind the counter, in the open entrance to the kitchen, another body sprawled over the flooring. A soaked apron clung to the corpse. Sopping wet clothes saran-wrapped the outline. Flayed flesh hung in flaps from the body. No skin remained. Chunks of yellow connective tissue and fat shone on the body like wax and shimmered in the light.

Then, the smells registered in his nostrils. From the back kitchen, high, overwhelming burning filled the air of food left in the fryers, decimated to crisps. Blackened bacon, sausage eggs, coffee, toast, and rank, putrid decay, rotting, miasma swelled. Copper blood, excrement, ammonia, sulfur, methane filled the diner. The smells of rot, decay, and gore distended in the air, the restaurant pregnant with it.

Matthew's stomach lurched and his mouth opened. A whoop of air sucked in through his lips, his chest hitched, and wind whistled in and out. He screamed and the sound echoed in the confines of the diner. The muscles in his neck balled and his vocal chords scraped and he tasted blood. The thick warm-penny smell filled the back of his nostrils, and his vision grayed. His eyes took in the scene before him and all logic failed. His mind froze and he screamed again.

32

Michael's head throbbed, his body ached, and his vision remained an unending, perfect field of black. There was nothing but the steady thud of his heart in his head. Pounding, pounding, pounding. He pressed his hands against his ears, but the sounds had faded. Then, there was quiet. His hands remained and his eyes clenched shut. He didn't know how long had passed before his eyes opened again, but when he did, his body shivered. His clothes clung to his sweat-glazed body, frozen. His breath fumed out before him in a cloud and his teeth chattered. He lowered his hands from his head and wrapped his arms around his body, curling himself against the far wall. The screaming was gone. The screaming had left and now it was quiet. On the floor before him, his eyes slunk to the spatter of curds. White, coagulated pus, sharp brown shell jutting from the mess. The line of gunk had frozen to the ground.

A migraine pulsed behind both of his eyes. It

was quiet. God, it was quiet. Finally, quiet. Tears erupted from him and his body convulsed with sobs. His head collapsed into his lap. He pressed his eyes against his knees.

"I love you, daddy."

"I love you, too, Dylan."

"There's always the chance that your son finds his way back home. I'd suggest someone stay at the house, along with one of our officers, in case he comes back. Perhaps your wife would be best."

"I love you, Michael."

"I love you, Lisa. To the moon and back."

"To the moon and back, Michael."

Every muscle in his body clenched. His fingernails felt as if they were pulling away from the beds. Feeling waned in his fingers. His toes were distant and numb. Both of his feet were cold blocks. Hot lines of tears slipped from his eyes, nipped his skin, and crusted his cheeks. Despite them, his eyes felt bloodshot and dry. Hurt. Everything hurt. Every part of him throbbed, aching and weak. His body quivered in the cold of the freezer.

Then, the screaming began again. A sharp noise, he heard it even through the metal of the freezer door, the vault before him, sealing him off from the outside world. The scream pierced through the barrier and rose to his ears. A maddening yell of despair, of insanity, of disbelief. A human cry. But not the chittering that rose before. No. Not yet. Michael listened as the scream ran out, and there was a pause, a break of inhalation, before the high, horrible whistling, human yell began again, and Michael shambled to his feet and burst forward from the sealed freezer door.

33

If he hadn't gotten off work late, he wouldn't have been where he was, when he was, and the question it all came down to was: was there any purpose, or was it all a game of luck, a game of chance? Was it all just a crapshoot with no meaning?

No words passed between them. In the front passenger seat, incredibly, the older woman had fallen asleep. Her head laid resting against the seatbelt. On the window, he could see her breath on the glass, minutely fogging it with each exhalation, before inhaling and erasing it. His foot hadn't left the gas.

His name was Roger Bellcrest. He was fifty-four years old. He had been married once, for four years, before his wife left him for another man. He'd always been faithful. He'd never hit his wife or spoken foully to her. He never found another woman to share his life with. As time passed, he found he enjoyed the company of himself more than anything. Although he'd assumed several jobs throughout his life, most recently, he'd worked as a cryo driver, delivering CO_2 and Hydrogen. He worked for a long time on the road pulling hard shifts and long hours. Recently, however, he'd secured a gig where he solely did local jobs. The long trips disappeared and he worked with men who repped the same amount of experience as he. It was a position he knew he'd retire in. He could retire early with great benefits and a steady plan. Then, the world changed.

He clocked out that evening, but couldn't remember the time. He remembered leaving the office, saying goodbye to Seymour, punching out, and getting in his truck. He remembered stopping to get gas on the way home, checking his tires while at the pump, and the pressure on all of them reading 32 with his manual gauge. He remembered that he stuck his wallet back in his front pocket as the pump clicked off and when he printed his receipt. Always his front pocket. When he was 13 years old, he'd had his wallet stolen out of his back pocket, downtown, and hadn't discovered it was missing until hours later. He'd been on a date then. He remembered that. On that date, he discovered that his wallet was stolen when they got something to eat and she reached into the back pocket of his jeans only to discover air. Empty air.

He remembered sticking the receipt the pump

spit out into his middle console as he got back in the truck. Then, driving. Driving home. He'd taken the long way home–take the long way home, there was a song, he was sure of it, that he remembered– because the night was beautiful. He rode with the driver's side window cracked. Warm air whistled in the cab and he watched the lights pass over as he crossed MLK bridge, the streetlamps raining down in waterfalls of orange. Waves bathed the truck as he passed under each lamp. The sounds of the city settling down flowed into his vehicle. He remembered feeling the most relaxed he had in a while while driving down the boulevard and peering at the buildings overhead. The giant structures, glass outlines against the sky, stretching high, stretching above made him feel small. They reminded him of how it really was, how little he was in the grand scheme of things. The thought brought only peace, no discomfort, no displeasure, no anxiety. He drove as he thought of the breeze, thought of the night, the air, the bleeding amber orange lights from above, the dark reflection of his vehicle as it blurred by in the polarized glass windows of the buildings and towers. He saw the lone woman. No one walked the sidewalk but her. She strode alone, sad and alone. As he came closer, he saw tears lining her eyes. He stopped and picked her up, but then all memory blurred and nothing seemed straight. He remembered her, but the line faded. He remembered peace, then picking her up, but as he thought of what connected the two memories, he ran only into cloud. A dead-end. A bar of striped yellow and black. A red STOP sign. The road washed out and all memory ceased. Then, she was with him, crying. He remembered her crying, the pain in her eyes, and he remembered driving them both away. He remembered how much she reminded him of his grandmother, who had been dead decades. His grandmother Rosemary, who loved him, raised him, saw him through highschool, and took care of him.

But nothing remained for the time. The gap gaped. The persistence of memory faded into oblivion and it was like seeing in the dark. The feeling of going to the restroom with the lights on, turning them off as you leave the room, watching your vision become black in an instant, and suddenly forgetting where everything was, even though it once existed and was once visible only moments before.

Roger drove as the old woman slept in the passenger seat as he coasted the highway and tried to remember. There was darkness, but in the darkness, he remembered it moving. He remembered movement, dark movement, and chittering, gnashing of teeth—*But the children of the kingdom shall be cast into outer darkness...there shall be weeping and gnashing of teeth*—and horrible noises. Horrible chattering of a thousand mouths moving and screaming, screaming, the mouths screaming. He remembered darkness. He remembered the gas station, driving away, and then something happening. Not picking the old lady up. Not immediately. He remembered the night, the—*dark*—night, the wind, the breeze, the lights, the city, downtown driving. Before he saw her, the old lady, he remembered something happening, seeing something, something—*And he opened the bottomless pit*—moving down the side of the street. A flood. A burst fire hydrant. A wave of dark and from—*there arose a smoke out of the pit, as the smoke of a great furnace*—the flood there had been gnashing, screaming—*and the sun and the air were darkened by reason*—and he remembered smoke rising, smoke rising from a car crashed into a building. He remembered the engine on fire. Great, black, billowing smoke rising from it and yellow-orange flames licking up the sides. Shattered glass shining like sequins on the sidewalk, throwing back the reflection of the flames. The smell as he sped by. The smell, the smell. Burning gasoline and charred meat. Crisp, black scents of pork and burning fat that flowed through his window, and the sequins of glass. Oil drops, black emeralds, and the smell of rot, stinking decay, death. Death and the flow of oil from the holes in the ground.

Manholes, they call those manholes.

Yes, and they had been opened, the covers removed, pushed off and thrown to the side, one after the other, like opened cavities, gaping mouths.

Like Pandora's box.

Like toothless mouths, vomiting up the flood, the moving water, the living oil, the millions of shining droplets, gemstones that crawled and twitched and flowed.

He remembered more cars and trucks and the outlines of drivers and passengers. He remembered running and driving and sweating and screaming. He couldn't remember if his mouth opened or if the screaming had been in his head, replayed on loop, again and again, as the smoke rose around him and nothing else came. Only the smells and smoke. Burning death. Smoke and fire and–*ashes to ashes, dust to dust*–death, horrible death, the smell of death and then...the old woman. Nothing else (*I know who I was when I got up this morning, but I think I must have been changed several times since then*). He knew he stopped. He knew he picked her up, but there was nothing else. Only the smells and darkness. Fragments, glittering pieces, sinking in the murk of his mind, falling away, washing apart as he tried to grasp them. There was nothing. Nothing. Only the sounds and the smells and fear, deep fear, that refused to leave him.

His eyes watched the road ahead, the woman slept, and he continued down I-44 away from the fear. Driving. Driving. Driving towards memory, away from what laid behind them, with the woman in his car (*somehow you strayed and lost your way, and now there'll be no time to play*). He gripped the wheel and his knuckles stood out white (*no time for joy, no time for friends*). Roger drove and (*–not even time to make amends*) recalled the noises, the sounds, and what happened to the world behind them. The woman slept and the wheels rolled on. As the miles grew, his memory surfaced again.

34

The world had fallen, finally, and the moment he knew was coming– the day that had been predicted, long ago, centuries before– had finally come. Lindsey supposed some of them had been right. The Mayans, the Aztecs, the ancient civilizations. The end times didn't come biblically. There was no war, no man-made disaster, no rise of the antichrist. No souls were lifted up to Heaven, none were in the field, one taken, the other left, no floods, nor catastrophic storms, nor geo-nuclear explosions had shaken the earth, but in a strange sense, the 2012 prediction was almost apt. A reckoning had come. The earth had opened up, and from the crust spilled forth the end. The flood that would cover the earth again, and kill every living thing. The plague of end times. There were no cicadas, but insects had come. Lindsey had seen it. He watched it happen. Endless insects. Endless bugs. Their day on the earth was over. For humanity, their day had come, and their time in the sun was finished. It had been a good run, but perhaps, enough was enough.

He thought of everything that was coming to an end, as his breath grew shallower. He was hot, so hot. Perhaps, it was just as well that the whole thing had happened. His breath juddered from him as he cackled a laugh–a lunatic cry– and felt resigned tears rise in his throat, then to both of his eyes, choking. This was how the world went. This is how it ends. Not in an explosion, but in a quick and lethal death, and that much he could only assume.

He pressed the power button on his phone and glared at the screen. No service. No internet. Nothing. In his hand, he held his lifeline, and the connection had been cut, and that was how he knew it was the end. Everything was spoken by the device. By those two words in the top right-hand corner. Despite all the other questions that rose to his mind–the other possibilities– he didn't forget checking his phone an hour before. Right before the end had come, he'd seen the same NO SERVICE message, so little, yet so big on the illuminated face of his phone. NO SERVICE. If tragedy struck the way he wished it would have, with everyone's pants down, where no one knew what was going on, while the Captain and passengers alike went down with the ship, holding one another, crying, all in the same situation, understanding that there was nothing that could be done, and that they were simply already dead– there would still be service. There would exist the possibility to phone someone for help– for those who had survived– to video, to record, to export information, spread the news, call mayday, but nothing worked. For that, in the bottom of his heart, he knew someone knew. Someone knew the end was coming and tried to stop it, or was actively trying. And that included not merely stopping whatever hell had arisen from the earth from getting any further out–from spreading–but from stopping any and all information from getting out, too. What better way was there to do so than by cutting all communications?

I'm sorry sir, but your party can't be reached, he thought and laughed again, but couldn't tell anymore if he was laughing or crying. His voice came out hoarse and torn from his throat, from chapped lips and a mouth as dry as cotton. The inside of the safe grew hotter and hotter still and sweat pooled beneath him. His shirt paper-mâchéd to his back. Rivulets ran down his spine, over his tailbone, and between the cleft of his buttocks. Here he was, safe from it all.

SAFE! GET IT, LINDSEY?! GET IT?!

He barked another shallow-breathed laugh and

tears dripped down his cheeks. His nose ran and his eyes stared at the dark, black velvet of the safe enclosing him. His crypt. His tomb. His 11 gauge steel, 10, ¼" thick locking bar, 5-foot-tall coffin. 110 minutes of fire protection, lots of storage for up to–*believe it or not, folks!*–an impressive 45 individual long guns, and removable shelving, customizable to each and every owner's storage needs. Level 5 security, designed by the very best, for the very best. He would never forget the sound of the electronic lock clicking shut behind him as he slammed the door on himself. The irrevocable slick, shushing sound, then the forever *click* of the bars sliding home.

Only the very best, sir.

He remembered the day he bought the safe. How proud he had been. How pretty of a penny it had cost. He remembered the sound of the bugs. Their screech as he ran, as he darted from the kitchen, where they overflowed from the sink, filling the stainless steel basin, and gurgling up, crawling everywhere, in an endless tide. In that split moment, he had gone for his closet– *Your closet, why your closet, Lindsey? Why there?*– and keyed in his code, and threw the shelving to the floor, tossed aside his guns, tore everything out, and slammed himself into the metal container, heaving the door shut behind him as the black wave followed him into the bedroom, covering everything in an endless torrent.

He remembered watching the walls and the flooring disappear, before the steel shut closed and it all became black, the light and air shutting out, alike. The door crashed closed and the locks shot home, and darkness enveloped him in a blanket, a cocoon, and the screams raged. Outside the safe, as he shut himself inside, he heard the roar of the insects, as if they knew, as if they understood that they had been thwarted–*as if they fucking understood*–and he pressed his hands against his ears as hard as he could, shut his eyes and hoped, prayed that they couldn't find a way in, that there was no crack or seam they could squeeze through, pry between, and eviscerate their prey, trapped in the box. But there was none. The safe was foolproof, airtight, and that was the comedy of it all. Fate had given him two options: the insects or the box– and he had chosen. So, now he suffocated slowly, pouring sweat and inhaling more and more carbon dioxide with each breath, and laughing and crying.

When life gives you lemons, he thought and wheezed, his throat a pinhole. Every breath felt shallow, short.

You're dying, Lindsey. This is what it feels like to die. Houdini may have made it out of the milk can, but he couldn't escape fate, either. It gets everyone, in the end.

Eventually the screeching of the bugs ceased and silence enveloped the house again. He doubted they still lingered outside the safe, yet no doubt laid in his mind that if he opened the door again, they would hear and come crawling back. But such a contingency was nonexistent. Lindsey wondered if anyone else was still alive, or if their fates had already been sealed. Perhaps there were others waiting for the end to come, just like him. Perhaps it was all over for everybody, the punch-outs on the eternal time cards differing only by hours, minutes. Perhaps the show was over and whoever was in charge was only waiting for the theatre to clear out. Thank you everybody, goodnight.

Lindsey picked up his phone and pressed the power button on the side. The phone face lit up dully, the brightness turned down. The time read 9:37 p.m. Monday, June 9th. 82% battery. A near full charge and no one to call.

All dressed up and nowhere to go.

His lips split apart in a humorless smile. As he swallowed, his throat clicked. It felt like swallowing a handful of buttons. He let his phone drop to the floor of the safe and leaned his head against the wall. A headache pulsed behind his eyes. He closed them and his vision, unchanging, remained black. Darkness to darkness. Hot air cramped him.

A thin trickle of sweat jetted down his chest, into the waistband of his pants. The end had come for him. Lindsey closed his eyes and waited.

35

Robin clutched his orange crayon in his small fist, holding it tight against his chest, but careful in his fingers, so as not to break it. The paper wrapper darkened with moisture from his slicked palm. His hand hadn't unfurled since he grabbed it.

He stared at the walls around him and huddled into himself in the corner, shivering in the cold. It was so dark and so quiet and he was tired, so tired. His arms wrapped around his body but provided no warmth. His pajamas held no heat in. There was no feeling in his toes.

The sounds had stopped and he wanted to leave. He wanted to get out, to go, to see his mommy again, but she had told him to stay and to not come out, no matter what. So, he stayed. He didn't move. He wanted to see his mommy and he wanted to see his picture. He looked down at the crayon in his hand and thought of his picture. An orange lion, under a great orange sun. Orange was his favorite color because it reminded him of all of his favorite things. Orange soda, orange candy, the orange sun, Mrs. Rupert's orange cat, his mommy's orange purse, orange sherbet, the kind he always got when his mommy took him out to get frozen yogurt, whenever he was sick, had a bad day, or for a special treat.

Suddenly, his face crumpled and his hand tightened on his crayon. Tears welled up like a latex balloon in his throat. It became hard to breathe. His mouth opened and a sob like a bubble burst on his lips. Both of his nostrils clogged up and he sucked in his breath.

Don't cry, Robin! Don't cry! You have to be quiet! he told himself, and shut his lips tight to keep from making a noise. His chest hitched up and down and his cries shuddered down his back and his arms. His whole body quivered. He wanted his mommy. He wanted to see Mrs. Rupert's cat, Frida. He wanted to keep coloring his picture and hug his mommy and be warm. It was so cold in the fridge. He didn't know how long he'd been inside of it for. There was no way of telling. A few minutes could have passed, as easily as several hours, days, years.

I want to go home, he thought, and wanted to be back in his bed.

You are home, Robin, a voice that wasn't him answered. He felt like he was in a bad dream—*"You just had a nightmare, Robbie. It's not real, baby.*

It's okay. Mommy's here and nothing's going to get you"—and he wanted to wake up.

"If you ever have a dream you don't like, just think of a new dream and change the channel, like on TV."

Robin clenched his eyes shut. He thought of going to the zoo with mommy and seeing the lions sunbathing, going right up to the glass and watching the big cat roll over on his back to soak up the rays. He thought of seeing the orange monkeys (*Ooo-rang-uh-tans, the zookeeper had told him, and that one's name was Lucy, and they had her for about five years, now, and wasn't she beautiful?*), and the striped orange tigers, and butterflies landing on him in the enclosure and drinking gatorade from a clear-plastic dixie cup he and his mommy got when they came in. He thought of the orange sun, peeking through his window in the morning and his mommy waking him, to come eat breakfast, and drink his–*orange*–juice, and if he had enough time before school, he could watch a little bit of cartoons, then when he got home, some more if he got all his homework done. He thought of better dreams, better places, better things, happy things, and didn't notice his breath gradually growing shallower. He dreamed better dreams and thought of a wonderful, gray plastic remote, just like the one that went to the TV in his room. The small, square-box television set mounted in the corner with the built-in dvd player for all of his movies. His finger pressed on the channel button, flipping, scrolling through the stations, and on each one were things he loved.

Memories like orange marmalade melded thick and sweet in his mind's eye. He fell into himself and his waking thoughts subsided as he fell asleep against the wall of the fridge. His coldness turned to numbness, which slipped away from him and his dreams took over, warming him from inside as the world faded and all bad thoughts shed from him. Lost like stations, white noise static, gone in the haze.

36

At 7:34 p.m on Monday, June 9th, Belinda Lundy heard her son Robin call from the other room, stating that the toilet wouldn't flush, and sighed deeply at the prospect of having to call someone out for a clogged pipe. It wouldn't have been the first time they'd experienced issues with the rental since moving in, now, eighteen months before. She finished undressing from the day, removing her scrubs, throwing them in the dirty hamper she kept by the door, and changed into sweats before heading to Robin's bathroom. Her son stood barefooted on the tile, in his Spiderman Pajamas, with both hands planted at the base of his back. A smear of concern dabbed his expression. I'm sorry. I promise I didn't do anything, the look read and she believed him. Belinda first tried the handle and upon jiggling it, the toilet jogged, but no water drained down the pipe. The bowl began to fill and she grabbed the plunger from behind the toilet, shoving it down against the siphon jet. She pumped her arms a few times, when she finally felt something dislodge. She removed the plunger, the water level in the bowl sank, and dozens of black, metallic flakes fluttered up from the jet, splashing up against the sides of the bowl. They crawled over the porcelain, up over the lip, and Robin screamed. Hundreds, upon thousands of insects flowed up from the toilet. Instinct kicked in and Belinda grabbed her child and ran. As they dashed from the bathroom, a mad, subdued chittering, like cicadas, maracas, a box of rice krispies being shaken up and down, perpetually, endlessly, rose in the house and as Belinda carried her son, her eyes saw the same bugs gurgling up from the bathroom sink. When they made it into the hall, an impossible black wave flowed from the front door, closing them in. Again, in an instant, without thought, she dashed into the kitchen. From behind them, the oil spill closed in, covering everything and Belinda ran. Her eyes watched the walls of her home, the floors, the ceiling, become a living, twitching flesh. The skin of a black dragon, scaled, moving, breathing, rising and falling with each inhale. To the left, darkness enclosed her and her child and to the right, the black mass approached. From behind them, the unthinkable tide flowed unceasingly toward them. A circle formed around them and Belinda threw the fridge door open, ripping shelving out. Glass jars flew and shattered against the tiled flooring. Tupperware exploded against cabinets behind her and the home filled with the neverending screech, now an unbearable shrill scream, and the smells of death. Yellow, gangrenous, decay. Horrible death. Excrement, rot, and filth. Belinda shoved her only child in, her only true motivation for life, her only true love in the world, and held his face in her hands.

"Don't come out baby, no matter what. Stay in here, no matter what."

She kissed his forehead and shoved him inside, making sure the door sealed again, before slamming her back against the stainless steel. She made no noise as the circle closed and consumed her. Her jaw locked and no sound escaped her. Even in death, her maternal instincts took hold. She refused to let her son hear her cries.

By 7:59 p.m. there was nothing left of her. Minutes later, the chittering ceased entirely and the horde moved on.

Robin survived for a little over five hours in the fridge.

37

Colonel Harland Quiver looked at the file on his desk once more, set it down atop the polished wood surface, pushed his chair out, and sat in the diffuse light of the lamp. The phone stood beside the file like a sentry, once active, now resigned to watching, waiting, and anticipating the moment to fire again and ring, delivering orders like bullets from one side of the nation to another. One connection to another. Operator A to Operator B, then Operator B to Operator C, and finally Operator C to Operator D. Each entrusted with a set of codes, providing a triple blind, so no one person knew what each one meant. Only the first and final parties knew. Communication A to communication D. But there were no more messages to be delivered. The decision had been made, and Colonel Quiver, his eyes stuck on the plain, cream colored plastic receiver and handset, knew the implications. The final executive order had been made by the highest chain in command,

and there was nothing left to do. The president had spoken.

Harland rested his hands in his lap and let his eyes stray from the phone to the door before him to his office. The only entryway and exit point to the room, this room, somewhere meters upon meters under the surface of the earth, in an undisclosed location in America. Somewhere unsuspecting, hidden, furtive. Right beneath the noses of the American public. Just as all their work always was and always would be. He had believed in its purpose once, the logic of their ways. There were certain tasks that need not be known by the American public, if the objectives were pure, righteous. There were certain methods that the general public didn't need to understand if the means justified the end–if the outcome brought a greater good for the greater good. Harland once believed that. He bought in fully to the ideology, and now, if questioned, he couldn't answer why. He believed it because he wanted to believe it, just as every person doing a difficult job wants to believe. They want to believe that they're doing the best they can given the circumstances. He had, truly, but he failed in his purpose and no longer believed. The decision had been made. Despite all of the advice he provided, he'd had no say. The decision had been made and he failed to protect the lives he was enlisted to guard.

Thirty eight years of service. His country had saved him. He dedicated his life to it and had failed it. From humble beginnings to Secretary of Defense, Harland never forgot his roots, never forgot the farmhouse he grew up on, the smell of country, dirt, sweat, and hard work. He never forgot blistered hands, tears of pain, or defeat. He never forgot the sorrow of the continuous cycle of not being able to do enough to get by and he never forgot the opportunity his country provided him to escape, and to send money back home by enlisting, and the hard work, respect, and gratitude it taught him. He never forgot the molding of his mind and body that it crafted, making more than a man out of him. Making a fighter for those who couldn't fight for themselves. Making a guardian for those who had none. Making a protector for those without aid. Making a harbinger of peace for situations that held none.

You take pride in your country, Harland. You understand how lucky you are to've been born here. Never forget the people who died for your rights, his grandpa's voice echoed, ripples in the waters of his memories, a veteran of his own right. Twenty years of active duty in the Air Force. His own father had served five in the Marine Corps before dying overseas. Bradley Quiver, recipient of the

Purple Heart for bravery in Iraq, when after striking a land mine in the truck he was driving, he managed to deliver the survivors of his squadron to the next safety point, before bleeding out.

He never forgot. He worked, served his country, served his family, and did the best he could to bring peace, to avoid any and all casualties, and to harbor peace. Peace was the key. The preservation of any and all life, the utmost priority. That was what he had been told his whole life, his whole career, and he believed it. God, he believed it. He believed that was the utmost priority of his country.

His eyes fell to the report on his desk again as he leaned forward in his chair, before coming to a stand, crossing the small twenty-by-twenty-foot room, and turning the lock on the door. He about-faced and walked back to his desk, the small camera mounted in the corner of the cold, metallic cubicle office watching his every move. His dress shoes clicked over the concrete flooring. Nothing decorated the walls. No windows let light in. Only a row of lights above and the small lamp on his desk could illuminate the space. The lights stayed off. In the isolated room, only the polished wood desk, the single office chair, the lamp, and Harland occupied air.

Harland found his way back to his chair again, opened the lower drawer of his desk, and took his service revolver from inside. He removed the magazine, checked the rounds and the chamber, replaced the magazine, took off the safety, and cocked the revolver. His eyes flitted from the file, to the small red dot of the mounted camera, blinking, observing. Everything recorded and monitored. In the hallway, he heard hurried footsteps already. Then, he leaned back in his chair, stuck the gun against the ridge of his jaw, and pulled the trigger.

38

A distressing clunking sound emitted from the Chevy. Its continuation broke her from nothingness and reeled her back in. She glared through the windshield, looking past the dark droplets that had dried on the glass to splotches of black ink. Her fingers ached on the steering wheel, each hooked around the leather grip. The muscles in her back and arms cried out. The clunking grew louder and the red arrow on the fuel gauge sunk below E. On the passenger seat beside her, her phone laid, unused, disconnected, a worthless appendage.

"Okay. Just be back by eight. That's reasonable enough, isn't it, Sabrina?"

She left that night in a fight with her mother, her father in the kitchen finishing up the dishes from dinner in the sink, her brother helping clean the table off and load the dishwasher.

"No, it's not. It's ridiculous," she spat and stood with her hands on her hips, her phone in her hand.

"It's a weeknight and I think that I'm being more

than generous with you, sister."

"No, you're acting like I'm still a child."

"Honey, your father and I aren't trying to be unreasonable. We only want what's best for you"

Silence came from the kitchen and she knew her brother and father were listening and that made her madder. Her jaw tightened.

"I wish you would trust me more," she said.

"We do, Sabrina, and we're trying, but you're still our baby and it's always going to be hard for your father and me to let go."

And in that moment, with her frustration swelling, she let her anger speak.

"I wish you would."

She stamped to the front door and saw her mother's hurt frown as she turned away. She twisted the deadbolt and stepped outside.

"I love you Sabrina," her mother said and she shut the door and left.

Fresh tears sept from both of her eyes. The clunking in the car thunked again and again with the turning of her wheels, and without her taking her foot off the gas any, her speed decelerated. The motor whined and sputtered and she watched, her attention hooked by the Chevy, as the speedometer dropped from 60, to 50, to 40, and the gas stopped working. With the pedal fully depressed, the vehicle coughed into neutral and coasted over the country blacktop. Her momentum carried her and the speedometer crept lower. 30. 20. 10. The Chevy rolled over the two lane highway and she steered around a slight curve, before the road straightened out again. She took her foot off the gas as the needle hovered below 10, then sunk to the single etch before 0. To both sides of her, trees enclosed the highway. Beyond the wall of greenery, she could see nothing. Above, in the sky, the moon watched, a cataractous, dispassionate eye.

The car rolled, crawling forward and Sabrina's hands released from the wheel as it stopped. Her fingers unfurled and the tendons in them cried as she straightened them. Over the highway, her headlights flooded the asphalt with soft white. She turned her key from the ignition and let it drop to the floorboard. The interior lights of the vehicle came on. Her eyes fell to her feet. From between them, her keychain winked light back up at her, a small, metallic turtle, studded with pink and purple jewels. She'd gotten it on her last family vacation to Dauphin Island.

Sabrina opened her car door and the warm summer night air swept her like smoke. She stepped one foot onto the road. Her leg buckled beneath her and she grabbed the car door handle, collapsing. Unnoticed pain lightninged up her legs as her knees connected with the ground. She pulled herself back up to a stand and trickles of warmth ran down her shin. Stinging called mutely from each leg. She stepped forward. Behind her, light bled from the car outwards. The door hung open. She circled to the hood. In the woods around her, katydids and crickets chirred, their sound riding the wind, shushing through the trees.

Her vision became a kaleidoscope of color, fragmenting into shards as she staggered forward. She wept and thought of her mother and her father and brother. One foot followed the other forward.

Just keep going, Sabrina. Just keep going, baby, her mother spoke in her ear, in her head, and she staggered forward, knowing they were behind her, nowhere ahead, knowing she had left them.

You left them, her mind spoke. *You left them, Sabrina.*

The rubber soles of her Vans scraped over the ground. She continued forward and each lift of her leg hurt, each placement of her foot back down howled. The tendons in her calves screamed, the muscles balled. Blisters that had formed on her heels and toes rubbed, back and forth, and sweat sept from her in sheets.

Just keep going, her mother said again.

It's okay, Sabrina, her father spoke. *It's okay, sweetheart.*

You left them to die. You left them alone, her mind

said, and she saw her mother and her father and her brother in the kitchen, desecrated, maimed. She saw their mangled corpses mutilated beyond recognition. She saw their outlines, before the end, pulsing, writhing, screaming under the blanket of black, under the millions and millions of bugs crawling over them. The living tide. The pulsating mass. The knowing wave.

You left us to die, Sabrina.

She saw their corpses, their bodies, their outlines rise from the asphalt before her, draw from the shadows and seize and twitch.

It's your fault we died, Sabrina, they spoke at her from under the tide, and their voices coalesced into horrific harmony with the chittering of the bugs, the neverending chittering.

"No," she said and shook her head. Both of her hands hung, numb, by her sides. "No," she cried and her nails dug into the soft of her palms.

It's okay, her father said, a black cardboard cutout, standing before her, a retinal stain. *You'll join us soon, Sabrina. You'll be with us soon, sweetheart.*

It only hurts for a minute, her mother stood beside him and the outline of her brother. *That's reasonable enough, isn't it, Sabrina?*

Pins and needles dug into her spine and she shambled forward, blind, unseeing of the line of black SUVs blocking both lanes of the highway. Three vehicles in total parked horizontally across the asphalt. Windows like ink blotted each. No drivers were visible. Only three men positioned within the vehicles stood, sticking out the sunroofs. Black helmets and vests adorned each man. Goggles gave them the eyes of insects. Two of the men held black carbines. The last held the grip of a long barrel, connected to a hose that ran around to tanks on his back.

Voices came, but Sabrina heard none of them. One of the men spoke through a megaphone and the noise came garbled, like the noise from the trees, the crickets, the katydids. Behind her, the headlights of her Chevy illuminated her steps and she staggered forward, unrelenting. The voices grew louder and Sabrina saw her parents smiling, now as they were, as they should be. Their smiles glowed in the dark. They hugged one another and beckoned to her.

Come home, Sabrina. Come back home, sweetheart. Please, don't leave us again.

She wept and shambled forward in a broken run and the megaphone voices, alarmed, raised and raised and finally stopped. The megaphone dropped and a simultaneous clicking sound cracked through the air.

"Stay where you are, I repeat, stay where you

are!"

Come home, Sabrina, her father smiled and extended his hand for her. Her brother waited for her. Her mother.

A loud crash of sound, bright, white lightening and thunder ripped out. Sabrina felt the breath punched from her, as warmth exploded twice in her chest. She dropped to her knees, and a star exploded again before brilliant, burning white warmth–heat, pure heat–bloomed at the base of her throat, her neck. Her vision swam with the brilliant light and her breath stopped. She tried to pull air in and thin, gurgled whistling wheezed in her ears.

Then, a spark appeared in the darkness, a beautiful sputtering orange flame, and the sun swelled. Light, gorgeous, orange-yellow light swallowed her vision and the warmth grew. Brilliant, bright light filled the world, and fire consumed her entirely.

39

Desmond Sturgis pressed his left foot against the door, letting his boot rest on the lower compartment. Wads of paper, receipts, junk jutted from the opening. Stuff he needed to throw away. The truck needed cleaned out, deep cleaned, if truth be told. He supposed he'd get around to it sometime soon. Just as likely though, he wouldn't.

Add it to the list, he thought and chuckled, tapping his fingers on the steering wheel. Donald Fagen hummed from the speakers and a nice fine buzz swam in his head. There was no clock on the dash to tell the time, but if Desmond had to guess, he'd gamble it somewhere between nine and ten in the evening. Without any work tomorrow, he couldn't really give a good goddamn. He didn't have to. When he got word from on high that Chuck would be able to come in after all, his foreman, Bob Placker, told him to stay home.

"Got no sense in paying two assholes eight hours, for a job that barely requires one."

That had been fine by Desmond, fine like honeysuckle wine. The first place he went when the clock struck five was *Otto's Place*. There, he christened his good fortune with two beers to start. Then, another following, one more to make it even, and one for the road, paying for them all with the forty dollars in his wallet that'd been burning a hole. He didn't mean to drink as much as he did. When he arrived at *Otto's*, Otto himself had been there, his kid Ronnie to boot, and conversation came easy and nice. With Otto behind the counter, too, Desmond never found his hand with an empty bottle. After catching up and chatting (Desmond had known Otto and his family since primary school; he was an artifact, his bar, a landmark) and nearly falling off the stool in laughter once or twice. Otto's kid Ronnie, fresh out of high school and quick as a whip, was the funniest son of a bitch Desmond had ever encountered. His age always surprised him whenever he said it aloud, no matter how many times he heard it. Desmond finally said enough was enough, and only a handful of coins were left to shove back in his jeans pocket. Obligatorily, Otto asked him if he was okay to drive and Desmond affectionately told him he was and to kiss his gold plated ass. Ronnie spouted off that if his ass was really gold plated, he would've left them more money, and although the bantering wasn't that funny, Desmond laughed and wheezed all the way out to his truck. He was feeling fine.

His windows cracked, he took in the warm night and took the backroad back home. Sweet summer crickets and katydids whirred, a symphony of sound carried far by the wind. Peepers croaked and called. The trees swayed back and forth, dotting the rural hillside. Both of his eyes drooped sleepily. He didn't realize how tired he was until hopping in the car to drive home.

Pent up, his mind offered and he took it, like a kid grabbing candy. Yeah. Pent up. Pent up stress, pent up frustrations. Tonight was the first night he really got to kick back and what do you know? When you finally get a chance to relax, the body can rest. It was the truth though. Whenever he was stressed, he always slept like shit, and if he didn't have a beer or two when he got off work or before he got home, he was liable to carry that stress right into bed.

That's why you've been so tired lately.

That was probably right, but the thought of a reliance didn't make him happy. Then again, one or two beers wasn't so much a reliance as it was a preference, but then again, one or two beers hadn't been the trend lately, and he knew. He was far from an alcoholic, but never too far away from it either, a fact the missus never failed to remind him.

His thoughts turned back to her. He hoped she wouldn't be sour with him when he got home. He hadn't called her to tell her that he wouldn't be coming home right away, but he hadn't told her that he'd be off tomorrow and could help with things around the house, and having him free to herself would surely lighten her spirits.

No guarantee though, he thought.

No guarantee, but maybe apologizing before laying on the good news would lay the groundwork for a happier outlook. If he was lucky and played his cards right, he thought maybe he could get some, and boy how he wanted her. Thinking of her and the curves of her body. In the past few years, she'd put on a few extra pounds in her behind and her boobs. She'd been self conscious about it, but Desmond had been nothing but assuring. He felt himself tighten like a rock in his jeans. She was beautiful, damn sexy, but damn fierce too, when she wanted to be. That was part of her allure, though. He loved playing with fire, even if that meant being burnt from time to time.

And even if it is your own damn fault.

And that was true too, but what was the saying about teaching an old dog new tricks? She sure tried to teach him, and he knew it was good for him– hell, he'd gotten better about leaving his socks around the house–but old habits die hard.

He hoped she'd let him share some of her warmth when he got home. How did Hendrix put it? He hoped she'd let him stand next to her fire.

Come on, baby, please, he thought and grinned. *Please, please me.*

His truck rolled down the highway and his headlights guided the way, two narrow, yellow beams penetrating the dark.

No dark like country dark, he thought peacefully and the smile stayed on his lips as he rounded a sharp curve in the road before evening out back onto a straightaway. In the middle of nowhere, America, his wheels glode quietly and alone, his engine an unnoticed footnote in the sounds of the forests and fields around. He leaned his head back against the rest and settled further into his seat. In another three miles or so, his turn would come up and he'd be home and back to his lady. His eyes darted to the glovebox. Maybe tonight was the night to give Marsha the surprise that he'd gotten her last week. In a small, velvet case sat a new 14k gold-platted pendant that he'd picked up one day in town, when he got off early. Marsha hadn't the slightest idea that he'd ever gone to get it. She never knew that he'd gone to Springdale last week, nor that he'd been sent home early for going over hours. If it got down to it, he figured she could've speculated that he should've been running long on hours, but then again, it was always a toss up for whenever Bob told them to come in late or leave early or just plain ol' don't show up.

That's the ticket, he thought, and again his mind caressed the smooth curves of her neck, her shoulder blades, her hips and her tush in her jeans, the way her mouth hung open, just barely, when he got her motor running. His mind filled with her and the feel of her. His smile widened into a beam at how happy she'd be when she saw what he got her. He wasn't perfect, but he tried, and he loved her more than anything. He knew she loved him too.

Desmond's eyes pulled back up from the glove compartment to see the two vehicles parked catawampus across the road.

"Jesus Christ!"

His foot slammed on the brakes and his tires skidded over the asphalt, screeching. The truck fishtailed and the tendons in his arms screamed as he grabbed ahold of the wheel and struggled to keep it straight. His heart jumped up into his throat and stayed there, thudding, choking off his air and pulsing up his head. He swallowed, forcing it back down, and had only seconds to look through the windshield. In the light of his high beams he made out two black Chevy suburbans, sparkling and brand new, as if they'd rolled fresh off the assembly line that night. Both of the vehicles parked diagonally, side by side, blocking both lanes, but ready to pull out in an instant. In both of the midnight editions, men in ink-colored tactical gear stood armed with guns. Each of their eyes glowed green. Atop one of the vehicles, a faceless soldier manned a mounted weapon with a hose that extended down into the suburban.

Jesus, that's a flamethrower, he thought as all men armed raised their identical M4s. A dozen green-dot eyes stared at him through night vision goggles. The man atop the Chevy took aim with his weapon and a flame plumed from the front of the nozzle.

I'm an American, went through his head and in unison the carbines all fired. His windshield exploded inward and bullets punched through the cab, tearing it apart. Fire spewed from the nozzle of the gun and the truck erupted in flames. The tires popped, one by one. Flames consumed the hull. Within seconds, nothing was left but burning remains.

40

The terminal stood near empty. The boarding door on Gate 10 shut and flight 19 had already pulled away from the jet bridge. Melanie turned and watched it in the distance as it sped down the tarmac before lifting off. Her favorite part of the job was always watching lift off, seeing the wheels separate from the ground, the plane rise and become airborne, jetting off into the sky, a physical anomaly. She never grew tired of watching the feat and seeing the critical point that should've been an impossibility. It made no sense that so many tons of metal could lift off into the air and soar the skies. Yet it did. Lift and aerodynamics allowed air to move faster over the top of the wings than underneath them, and lower pressure above the wings and higher pressure below them caused the upward force that defied gravity, yet despite the understanding of basic principles, seeing something in action was more than knowing. Seeing was believing and the sight of a plane lifting off the ground–seeing and knowing that so many passengers were riding inside the giant, metal bullet, lifting off into the sky and flying like the birds, but against odds, against nature–never ceased to amaze her. Flight 19 sailed further into the night sky and Melanie traced the aircraft with her eyes until ascended above her sightline, and disappeared from her view through the windows.

She turned back to her computer. Beside the keyboard, her notepad smiled up at her. *Mrs. Melanie Sue Lindwood* scrawled across the top in neat, cursive. Her eyes sparkled over her left hand. In another two weeks, it would be official. She would no longer be Ms. Melanie Sue Cass, but Mrs. Melanie Sue Lindwood, loving and doting wife to the wonderful Mr. Andrew Ray Lindwood. Her breath sighed out. There had never been a doubt in her mind that she would spend her life with anyone but Drew. He was a wonderful man and Melanie knew he'd make a wonderful husband and father. Her mind went back to the note he'd written for her on their bathroom mirror that morning, before heading to work.

You make my heart soar, Mel, jotted in dry erase marker, encircled in a giant heart with a cartoon plane drawn beside it. She vaguely remembered his lips against hers, and in the trenches of sleep, him kissing her goodbye when he left (*I love you so much, Mel. I can't wait to see you this evening, sweetheart*). The mirror was the first thing she saw when she got up to get ready for work. Beneath the message, he'd written, hastily: Left coffee on the pot for you. When she walked into the kitchen, her favorite mug waited, ready, beside the machine and happy tears filled her eyes with how much she loved him and how ready she was to be with him– *In tha eyes of tha Lawd and tha law*, she thought and laughed– and to spend their life together. What a beautiful life it would be.

Melanie shook her mouse to wake up the desktop and her monitor blinked back on, sleepily, before her login screen prompted her to input her password. Her fingers flew over the keys– *flew, haha, very funny, Mel*– and she hit enter before the lock screen blinked away and her session popped up. The gears in the computer turned and her pages reappeared and the wheels kept spinning as it struggled to load them. Finally, the browser went gray and a small message appeared in the middle of the screen:

No internet
   Try checking your network or reconnecting to Wi-Fi
   err_intrnt_dscnnctd

Melanie hit refresh and the same wheels turned before an identical message arrived on screen.

"Hm," she grunted and pulled out her Iphone to check if it was connected. In the top right hand corner, the typical pie slice of three white bars was missing and opposite it, to the left read: *No Service*.

No service? Melanie flipped to her settings and tapped on Wi-Fi, then Cellular. Nothing. Zilch. She set her phone down on the counter and peeked over her desk, down the long, stretching hallway. Nobody walked about. Only a handful of stragglers hung about the dozen gates of the airport. There was only one terminal, and unless you wanted to travel to St. Louis, this was the closest airport around, and a small one at that. The Wi-Fi could've gone out, she wouldn't put that past SGD National, but her service shouldn't have been out too. Her eyes searched around her, looking for someone to make eye contact with, to confirm that they were having the same issue, too, when the handset on her desk went off, making her jump. She picked up the receiver.

"Hey Mel, this is Angie. You having any trouble with connection? My terminal just shit the bed and my phone's showing absolutely nothing for service."

"I was about to call you myself. No, I've got nothing either," she said and watched an older man in blue jeans, Nike Monarchs, and a gray pullover hoodie sleep with his head leaned as far back as the terminal seating allowed. His thick hands rested on his lap.

"Go figure. Probably some technical error. I'll phone Brewer and see what I can find out. Call right back."

"Sounds good," Melanie said and hung up.

The old man began to snore and another younger passenger joined the chorus, slumped in a chair a few gates down from the old fart. The hooded geezer whooped in air, let it out in a snarl, and the young man followed suit, snarfing in air and whistling it out. A small smile lit upon her lips, but her eyes darted nervously about. She really needed her system up and running before the next boarding time began.

Count your blessings that you don't work somewhere like Chicago or Houston, she thought and couldn't imagine what it would be like for crap to hit the fan at a place like that.

She picked up her pen and looked down at her soon-to-be-married name, again. Her hand scripted the same careful, slightly leaning font and dotted the two letter *i*'s with hearts. *Mrs. Melanie Sue Lindwood*. She dropped the pen and smiled down at the pad.

A small sound rose in the air and she found

her ear cocking toward it. From down the terminal, nearer security, she heard a faint humming, ringing, like the sound of tinnitus. It reminded her of all the times her father would plug in his power drill battery when she was little and she would always complain that it was ringing. A sound which he never heard, partly because, she later came to postulate, his hearing simply wasn't as good as it was. The sound in the air then sounded exactly like that. Melanie squinted her eyes and listened to the static sound, the high pitched, almost whistling, and her brow lowered as the sound changed and grew louder. It was no longer a whine, but a jittering; a sound like swarming mosquitoes, or flies, or bees.

The sound grew louder and the older man woke up, his eyes blinking, as if he couldn't quite remember where he was, before hearing the sound, too. Confusion molded his features and he leaned forward in his chair, his eyes narrowing, his head tilting toward the sound, when he and Melanie made eye contact. Neither said anything, but the old man's face twitched and she read the expression perfectly: *You hear that?*

She did, and the sound kept rising, when they saw the first of the skittering shapes dash across the carpet and into the dead-end terminal.

41

Chett Engle finished plugging in the desired altitude, heading and speed into the flight deck, flipping the console and maneuvering the controls until the autopilot was ready. They were all set on their present course to DFW, and would touch down in another hour and forty minutes. From there, they'd have a brief layover before continuing on to JFK.

Chett unbuckled his belt and arched his back. It'd been a long day, a long week. Beside him, his co-pilot, Nicholas Reinard–a young kid, wet behind the ears, but someone Chett enjoyed flying with immensely– studied his actions with the intensity of a dyslexic trying to read.

Chett folded his fingers into one another and flexed his arms outward, cracking all ten digits at once. "What do you think, Nick?"

"Weather looks good. Should be a pretty easy flight. On the level," he said and looked to his captain for approval.

"I think so, too." He leaned back in his seat again and looked out the front windshield of the aircraft. The board glowed green. On the altitude indicator, the plane's wings hovered just above the artificial horizon as they climbed. He loved flying the 737 for its sheer beauty and amount of technology involved. The plane could pretty well fly itself, and the two large flight displays were a sight for sore eyes. Easy to read, easy to handle, and everything within grasp, from weather information to aircraft performance data, the power and smoothness of the aircraft assured Engle anytime he got to fly one. He loved feeling the Boeing respond to his every delicate command and being in control of such a powerful plane. His eyes flicked over the radar display and the PFD juddered and glitched. The image warbled, then steadied, and the EFB blinked black before coming back on.

"What in the hell?" Nicholas said and Chett stared at the panel. His hand reached out and toggled the switch to receive. No sound came to the cockpit. No voices. No ground control. He flipped it back to transmit

"SGD National this is Flight 19, over."

Nothing came through. He flicked the toggle and received dead air. Nicholas' breath sucked in through his lips. Chett held up a hand.

"SGD National, this is Chett Engle, pilot of Flight

19, requesting verification, over."

Chett flipped back to receive and waited, breath held, for the volley but nothing came. He checked the transponder and changed the setting to 7600, then flicked the toggle back to transmit. His eyes swept the radio and control panels. Nothing looked wrong. Everything was up and running, all was smooth, so what was going on? His mouth dried out as sweat ran down his face and dripped into his eyes. He blinked away stinging salt and wiped his hand absently across his head.

"SGD this is Flight 19, repeat, Flight 19. Come in, over."

The toggle flicked back to receive and silence spoke. Chett's hands trembled on the control wheel and Nicholas's skin pulled taut against his jaw. His skin took on the light, translucent color of cheese. He swallowed hard and his throat clicked.

"SGD, this is Flight 19. Come in, over."

Chett checked all of their equipment and Nicholas's hands dashed over the panel, flipping and testing. Something was very wrong. They needed to turn around. Captain Engle took manual control again of the plane and turned to Nicholas.

"Okay, sparky, we're on our own," he said and Nicholas nodded. His breath staggered from his lips in shaky breaths. "Hang with me, now," he said and began steering the plane in a slow arc, back around.

42

Exactly ten minutes and thirty eight seconds after flight 19 lifted off the ground and sailed into the sky, and approximately six seconds after captain Chett Engle discovered the radio in his aircraft inoperable, two F18 Hornets with four AIM-9X sidewinders took flight from an undisclosed base in an undisclosed state with the precise coordinates of Flight 19 programmed into their trajectories. Within five minutes, they reached Flight 19, just as captain Chett Engle finished turning the plane around with the intention of landing it safely back at SGD National with all twenty seven passengers aboard. Two radio transmissions went out, one from the first of the F18 Hornets and the second from base, confirming orders. Each Hornet fired a single off-boresight heat-seeking missile. Both missiles met successfully with their targets and captain Chett Engle's admirable ambitions became null. In the sky, a giant explosion rocked the night, rippling the air, effectively tearing the hull of Flight 19 in two. Of the two separated pieces, both, amazingly enough, landed within miles of each other. The first crashed into an isolated section of woods, just north of US 160. The second half, comprising the front section of the 737 and the cockpit, crashed into a cornfield south of highway 44, very close to the airport which it took off from. On the initial contact with the first half, almost every passenger was killed by the blast from the missiles themselves. For the second however, captain Chett Engle and copilot Nicholas Reinard, along with three other passengers, were alive to see their section of the plane crash into the ground. All were killed on impact. No one witnessed either impact and coverage of the event would never come, locally, or in any other bordering states. By 9:01 p.m., only an hour after Flight 19 took off, it landed again, in pieces, and the SGD National remained silent, with no other flights taking off.

43

Michael jerked down the handle and launched from the freezer. The door swung open and slammed against the wall. His gaze jettisoned down the back hall of the kitchen toward the front lobby. The man in the front, looked through him and his feet didn't move. His jaw worked up and down and Michael braced himself for another piercing scream to tear through the air, but only windless gasps came from the man. Both eyes rolled in his head like ball bearings, his fists clenched and unclenched by his sides, and spit dripped from his open mouth. A thin hissing began to rise in the diner and Michael ran forward.

He dashed over the tiled flooring and rushed toward the man, like a linebacker. His arms pumped up and down by his sides. The hissing rose to a trill, building in volume. It was coming from the lobby again. The bathroom. Michael grabbed the man's arm and yanked him forward. His eyes bulged from the front of his face and rolled toward his gaze. Michael grappled the man and he stumbled forward. He almost fell, but the man reached out and grabbed the corner of the counter, before they both toppled over. Gore squelched beneath the man's dress shoes as his foot slipped and his head turned toward the open mouth of the bathroom door as the chittering became a squeal, nails grinding across plates and chalkboards, a high powered drill boring through metal. The sound of grinding, tearing, splitting. A dark wave overflowed from the toilet and spilled from the sink. Thousands of bugs tore toward them and Michael heaved the man forward with him. His eyes stayed glued to the mass of insects, the living tide, flowing toward them, before finally pulling away. The man ran with him.

Michael ran with his arm under the man's shoulder and supported his weight. The man's legs seemed useless beneath him. He hefted them both into the kitchen, past fryers and sinks, back toward the open freezer. Thick, coagulated, greasy stenches of burnt food filled the air and the smell of death flowed into the diner. The wave screamed behind them. Michael dragged the man beside him and the man began to squeal. He flung the man into the freezer and his legs tangled beneath him. The man went sprawling on the floor, skittering, pushing himself backward into the depth of the walk-in and Michael threw himself against the freezer door. His fingers grasped at the handle and he heaved the door back toward him. The door swung wildly on its hinges and Michael saw the wave of insects bulge into the kitchen. A dozen broke forward and sprinted over the flooring. Michael slammed the door shut and sent home the latch. Behind him, the man found his voice and began to scream again. Outside the door, the insects wailed.

The man scrambled against the wall, slapping at himself, pulling his clothes, his mouth extended impossibly wide as he ripped off his shoe, then his sock, then clawed at his pants. The man tore off his belt and pulled his pants around his ankles. He thrashed on the floor and Michael saw as the man writhed. Blood soaked the man's pants around his ankles and Michael watched as a dark, brown lump moved beneath the man's skin, traveling up his calf to the base of his thigh. The man screamed and Michael saw the flesh of his leg bulge as the tumor pushed further and further up.

"GETITOUTOFMEGETITOUTOFMEGETITO UTOFME!" he wailed, before his words turned to inane screams.

Michael's eyes searched the room and landed upon one of the shelves. In the low light of the sealed freezer, an open utility knife gleamed atop a cardboard box of frozen home fries. He launched forward and grabbed it and dropped in front of the man. The veins in the man's neck pulsed against his skin and his entire head darkened into a deep red. His jaw clenched and beads of sweat rushed down his face. The collar of his shirt stained, wet. Both hands squeezed the flesh of his thigh, the fingers pressing in, digging into skin. His mouth opened again and another horrible scream wailed from him.

Michael grabbed the man's thigh and cut into him with the razor. The blade popped through his skin. Blood welled from the wound and he dropped the blade, gripping the meat of his thigh with both hands. He squeezed and pressed the moving lump toward the cut and it squirmed under his grasp. A suffocated hiss sounded out and the man screamed as the bug emerged and skittered over his leg. The insect darted up Michael's fingers and pain erupted as spines cut into his skin. He brought his fist down on the floor and the insect erupted in a stinking jet of white. Blood gurgled from the man's thigh. His screaming stopped and his head leaned back. A dark pool formed beneath the two of them.

Dark circles formed under the man's eye and every vein in his face became visible as the color of his skin hollowed. His breath wheezed from his chest in short gasps. Both of his arms dropped to his side and his hands laid limp on the floor, dipped in blood.

Michael's eyes dashed toward the door, watching it, waiting, listening to the scream outside. No bugs squeezed beneath the gasket or wedged between. The screeching continued. He turned back toward the man, whose gaze floated before him, glazed over. His back pushed up against the wall. Michael brushed the blade out of the way. Blood smeared his palms, stained his fingers. His eyes caught on the man's leg. Blood continued to seep from his wounds and the pool grew around them, a crimson mirror, fanning out under the freezer light. The man's breath shortened. Each inhale became shallow. His eyes glared ahead.

Michael watched the door and listened to the two sounds. The endless scream and the breath of the man beside him. In, out. On and on. Warmth seeped through his pants and turned cold against his skin. The blood began to gel on the floor around them. His breath fumed out before him and the cold swept through him.

In…out. He listened to his breath, the man beside him. In……out….and outside the door, the endless mass screeched, on, and on, and on.

44

Sergeant Wilcox scanned the road, his eyes like a hawk, searching for prey. He waited with his hands on his carbine, in front of the Suburban poised to fire. In the other two SUVs, the members of his patrol awaited the same. Kirby, Sullivan, Walsh, Richter, and Floyd. He knew none of them personally. Only their names. Each member took aim with their carbines atop the right and left vehicles. Atop his own, Sullivan waited behind him, manning the XL18. All information remained undisclosed except their position and objective. Form an impenetrable blockade. Two hours before, he had been woken up, flown to base, then given coordinates. An hour later, he and his squadron arrived at their position and followed orders: Let nothing through. Shoot to kill. If any vehicle comes near, eliminate the driver, neutralize the threat, and control burn. No questions asked. None granted. Now, they all stood ready to continue their jobs.

Sergeant Wilcox scrutinized the highway. Their vehicles blocked both lanes. Three separate cars littered the road before him, blackened and charred. Flames sputtered from a Honda accord. Paint bubbled and peeled. Not thirty minutes before, the gas tank exploded. Inside the cab, a burned skeleton gripped the wheel.

His eyes took in the damage, but he felt nothing. There was no room for interpretation. He was simply following orders and that was all there was to it. Nothing else needed to concern him. Their resolve remained absolute and their watch steadfast.

They were somewhere in Missouri, currently. They had a job. They were to carry it out and await further instructions. Wilcox eyed the gaping bullet holes in the three vehicles. In all of them, the windshields had been blown out. Glass and rubber littered the asphalt and the air was thick with the smell of burned gasoline. Nothing moved around them. The sounds of the countryside and darkness continued, unabated, unbothered by the events of the road and brought solace to him. Life went on. Katydids, crickets, and peepers whirred from the trees. To his left, forests extended, thick and grown out. He could see no end through them. To his right, fields extended. A silent farmhouse sat on one of the rolling hills and Wilcox had eyed it, waiting for a light to come on, willing it, mutedly, to illuminate, but since arriving, nothing had changed, nothing had moved, except the three cars before them.

A black pit formed in his stomach as he watched the farmhouse. Maybe they had caught wind of the sounds of their carbines, seen the light of the flames, and stayed hidden. Or, just as easily, whatever they were stopping on the highway from getting out, had already gotten the inhabitants of the house. There was no room for speculation, but Wilcox knew whatever they were blockading in was not good. Something beyond them had gone very wrong. He only hoped that what they were doing was stopping the spread, and that their efforts weren't futile.

Too little too late, Ross, his father echoed in his mind.

His eyes turned back to the road and his ears listened for the approach of vehicles, persons, threats. Amidst the symphony of the night, a new sound arose, layered between, but rising, gaining volume. His company raised their carbines, hearing it too, and Wilcox aimed his at the road, his eyes laser-focused. Through the lens of his goggles, the world glowed green. He looked past the cars and aimed his crosshairs. The noise grew into a buzz and his brow lowered under his helmet. It wasn't the sound of an engine, but an organic noise. Not the sound of machinery, but a growing hum.

Wilcox lowered his weapon to gaze over the sight. All other sounds fell silent and the whining drone climbed to a squeal. The grinding noise roared and nothing else sounded. Then, the troop saw what approached, and screams filled the night.

45

Commander Roy sat at his station with his deputy to his side and thought about exactly the conversation he'd had with his son that morning, over the gender of a certain cartoon character, Tweety Bird, when the warning sound went off. His eyes turned to Quentin Farrell. They made contact, both men nodded, and each picked up the emergency message action book.

From the console, the alarm rang, then the transmission.

beepbeepbeepbeepbeepbeepbeepbeepbeep

"GOLF. ALPHA. 2. 3. CHARLIE. HOTEL–"

35 characters jittered on its wavelength and they filled out their forms. Grease pencil smudges on laminated red sheets. The transmission cut off. End of message.

Commander Roy repeated the message as did Deputy Farrell and their books were traded. Both men read each other's work and their eyes met. No mistakes were made. They opened the emergency war safe and each man input their combinations. Roy dialed his first, then followed Farrell. The safe unlocked. Neither man knew the other's combination. Both located an envelope from inside with the first two characters from the transmitted message.

GOLF. ALPHA.

Roy and Farrell retrieved their envelopes, opened them, and extracted the plastic cookies. Both snapped open. The men's eyes glared at their forms and the cookies, comparing. Each of the five characters matched exactly, confirming this was not a drill.

Roy turned to Farrell and waited. His deputy nodded back to him.

"Message confirmed, sir."

"Message confirmed, deputy. Enter launch code."

"Entering launch code."

An authenticated order from the President of the United States had been given, based on the war strategy the Pentagon had issued. The two men stood up and went to their positions. On the clock, Farrell wrote the time. Effective immediately. Roy unlocked the butterfly valve and ordered Farrell to enter the six digit code. The deputy turned the thumbwheels, each containing sixteen characters. There were over sixteen million eight hundred thousand possible combinations and only one would work. They had six chances to enter the correct code. On the seventh, even if they entered the correct code, the whole facility would shut down. Farrell turned the wheels and the code went through.

The launch was authenticated. The launch time was written on the clock. The butterfly valve was unlocked.

On each of the men's displays, the computer took over and the same message blinked.

LAUNCH ORDER: CONFIRMED
  TARGET COORDINATES: CONFIRMED
  LAUNCH TIME: CONFIRMED
  MISSILES ENABLED
  LAUNCH TIME: 60 SECONDS

Their missile was going to fly. Farrell read off the orders from the computer. Roy listened.

"Roger, deputy."

The two men extracted their launch keys. They took them to their locks, eighty-seven inches apart, met eyes and nodded.

"Insert launch key, Deputy."

The two men inserted their keys.

"Launch key inserted, sir."

"Roger. On my count, rotate the launch key,

Farrell. 3…2…1…launch."

Both men turned their keys against the spring load and held them for five seconds. On their boards a green light came on.

LAUNCH ENABLED.

The launch sequence started and the missile would no longer take orders from either man. Battery activation kicked on and two twenty-eight volt DC batteries began charging with electrolyte. Twenty-eight seconds rushed by in a blink and the Accessory Power Supply Light came on.

The missile is totally independent of us, now, Roy thought and heard the rumbling shift from above as the blast door slid open. The bell went off. It went through the tipsy beam. Guidance Go. Full Diagnostic Check. Another three seconds passed by and Roy returned to his chair. A deafening buzzer alarm sounded. Liftoff. *God above help us, we have liftoff.*

Roy stared ahead at the panel. From the time they turned their keys to the time the missile was gone, elapsed to a grand total of fifty-eight seconds. Thirty-to thirty-five minutes later, some six thousand miles away, their target was going to disappear under a fireball four to five times hotter than the center of the sun, three to four miles in diameter.

"Commander, you've done your duty as ordered by the president," Farrell spoke, but Roy chose not to hear him, didn't respond.

He began closing the blast door and finishing his assigned duties. Above, they would have enough food and water to last them thirty days. The blast valve slammed shut. They were now on recycled air. It would take about three to four weeks before they started suffocating to death. Roy leaned back in his chair and stared at the single segmented message that occupied the center of his screen.

AWAIT FURTHER ORDERS

46

Roger drove and as he drove he thought of the consequences of everything, what had happened. Where were they driving? He didn't know. The miles ate away beneath their tires and the fuel in his tank slowly dwindled down and as the road continued, a terrible sense of uselessness crept into his thoughts. The world had died. There was no assurance of this yet, nothing concrete, but behind them, at least, Springdale had ceased. In the city and headed out, crashed cars and wreckage littered the roads. Bodies laid across the sidewalks. As they drove further and further away, the sights diminished but didn't disappear completely. Less cars surfaced on the road. Less collisions. No traffic. They were the only travelers on the highway for miles and miles. Darkness encapsulated them as they rode on, following only the stretching asphalt. Along their drive, a beacon of light lit up the countryside. A gas station had caught on fire and exploded. The woman beside him remained asleep as he drove past it. It appeared on the horizon, a burning, smoking spire of flames and then disappeared as Roger laid his foot heavier on the gas, pressing past it. Out front, the charred shells of two vehicles sat. One right before the collapsed storefront. The other, crushed into the once-standing station sign. Nothing of the station stood. Everything had fallen in on itself, burned, near-unrecognizable. Only the interstate road sign, some hundred yards before it indicated that it had once been a Shubert's Super Stop.

Roger drove. The longer he drove, the more he wondered if there was anything left. Perhaps this hadn't been an isolated event. Maybe the whole world had collapsed. Maybe man's time in the sun had finally ended, as abruptly as the dinosaurs, in one fell swoop. Maybe God had simply gotten sick of their shit and decided to just wipe the board clean again. He didn't know, but no other cars drove on the road. No other signs of life showed before him.

His headlights pierced the veil of blackness that the rural landscape draped over them. No light pollution contaminated the sky and the night sat like ink, impenetrable, pure. When the line of vehicles appeared on the road, Roger almost didn't believe his eyes. As he rounded the corner and turned back onto a straightaway, they appeared from nowhere in the dark. He jolted up in his seat and slammed on the brakes. The truck skidded to a stop behind the bumper of the first vehicle. Five more sat before it, crashed into one another. All were black and mangled. Roger caught control of his breath and listened to the steady wheeze of it, in and out from his lungs. Three SUVs parked horizontally across both lanes of the highway. Before them, another three cars had crashed into the sides of the SUVs. Pinned between a charred Volkswagen and one of the Suburbans was a body dressed in all black, helmeted and with weaponry. The body didn't move. Beneath the fender of the Volkswagen, Roger could make out the lower half of the body and saw it was no longer connected to the top half. Beside the Volkswagen, a Chrysler and a Ford had collided into one another, trying to break through the barrier of SUVs. Each of the vehicles had been burned out, set alight. Small flames danced from the carbonized corpses of each. Burned bodies occupied all of them. Another two vehicles rested on their rims behind the SUV pile up. Smoke danced from the smoldering wrecks. The road was completely blocked. To both sides of the highway, the shoulder fell off into deep drainage ditches.

Roger turned to the woman in his passenger seat. She sat awake, her eyes taking in the massacre before them. No emotion rattled her expressions.

"This is the end, isn't it?" she asked and Roger nodded.

He turned his key in the ignition and shut the engine off. The red arrow on the fuel gauge sat just above E. He stepped out of the vehicle. The sounds of quiet surrounded them. Above the low sizzle of the vehicles, nothing sounded. No crickets, no katydids, no peepers. Silence dominated. Roger closed his door behind him, guiding it shut and his passenger did the same. She circled around the vehicle and took his hand. Their eyes met and the woman looked to him.

"Something very bad has happened, hasn't it?"

Tears grew in her eyes.

Roger nodded.

"Will you keep me safe?"

Roger nodded and her tears flowed freely. Her mouth quivered but remained shut and he led the old woman to the shoulder of the road. He helped her along the railing and the two squeezed past the sweltering mound of crashed vehicles. Behind the SUVs, the road opened again, perfectly clear. No vehicles made it past the barrier.

He and the woman walked, hand in hand, in silence. Only their footfalls whispered over the asphalt, but no one heard them.

47

The man beside him was dead. Michael laughed into the cold darkness. An hour before the light in the freezer had gone out, but the screaming never ceased. The wailing outside the door. He could no longer tell if it was there or simply inside his head, ringing in his ears. The noise never ceased. They hadn't left. They knew he was here, now, and they were waiting, patiently waiting for him to come out or for him to die. The man beside him had stopped breathing. He could only tell by feeling the man's side. His body had gone cold and beneath them, the man's blood had frozen his pant legs to the floor. He tried getting up and found he couldn't, like a rat on a glue trap, a bug in a roach motel. Another weak cry of laughter spilled from his lips. Tears ran down his face. They hurt as they coursed down the cold flesh of his cheeks. Each left frozen trails on his skin. He couldn't feel his fingers anymore. The nails felt as if they were slowly separating from their beds.

All feeling left his toes. His feet were somewhere, far away, distant, and sensation in his legs were drifting away. All the heat in his body contracted inward, trying to preserve itself. But he felt so cold, so cold and so tired, and his thoughts drifted between sleep and waking.

Only I'm not sleeping, he thought, *I'm dying.*

Two's company, he saw the dead man grin in the dark, and he laughed again. The laughter turned into a scream of anguish as he saw the dead man's mouth open wide and his cold arm of dead flesh wrap around him and embrace him like a drunk, swaying with his buddy. *Two's company, Michael.*

The screaming continued and he thought of his son, his wife, his family, his friends, his life. A very similar thought of someone who was not twenty miles away from him, emerged in his head also. Someone he would never know, never meet, or even imagine. Another lost light in the dark.

This is the end, isn't it?

Yes, Michael, it is, his own voice answered and the laughter continued and the screams and the cries. If it had only occurred five months from now, he thought and laughed. Yes, if only, if only. The weather was beautiful. It was a beautiful summer. Perfect conditions for bugs. Michael thought of his sixth grade science teacher, Mr. Brown.

"Believe it or not, most insects enter a comatose

state below 50, where they cease movement and development...most cockroaches, in fact, die, when the temperature drops below 45, since cockroaches are cold-blooded and cannot regulate their own body temperature."

Winter began in November, but cooler temperatures, sometimes even in October. Three months is all it would've taken. In another three months, most of them would start to die. Michael cried.

"Whatcha buildin' there, buddy?"

"A sandcastle!"

"Mind if I help?"

"I'm going to play with Kenny!"

"Okay. Just right out front?"

"Yeah!"

"Okay, have fun. Don't go too far."

This was the end. This was the end and it had caught everyone with their pants down. Michael closed his eyes and focused on his son, focused on his wife, and focused on their warmth. The screeching continued but he forced the sound out and sunk deeper into himself, thinking of warmth. He thought of holding his son, wrapping him up and bringing him home from the hospital when he was born. He thought of his wife's smile and her arms around him and he fell asleep for the last time.

48

Roger's shoes scraped across the asphalt and his palm sweat inside the woman's hand. The road continued on. No cars. No people. Their feet moved beneath them and they walked, step after step. There was no destination. Only something to move from. Tears flowed numbly from Roger, as they did the woman, but the tears meant nothing to either of them. Neither felt them. Neither noticed. They only walked and looked ahead, for something, seeing nothing. Searching and wanting, but finding only blackness, darkness, silence, night. The woman faltered and dropped to one knee, her shoe catching on a divot in the road and Roger stooped, reaching beneath her arm to lift her back up when the darkness became light and the sky turned to white. Roger clenched his eyes shut. As the brightness faded, he turned and saw the night stained. A nova of pure brightness recoiled into itself and from the ground rose a pillar of light, fusing from white, to yellow, to orange, to red, rising into the sky. Fresh tears spilled from his eyes as incredible heat rushed toward him and the woman. His skin boiled on his face and his breath sucked from his lungs as sweltering wind consumed them. Then, the thunder of God rang through the night and the rising cloud became the last sight they saw as the force of the explosion tore through them, past them, and decimated everything that laid in its wake. The blackness of the night became light, and fiery destruction blazed, lighting all dark.

49

On every television in America that following morning, the same message played. Millions of eyes watched the screen, millions of mothers hushed their children at breakfast, millions of businessmen told their coworkers to be quiet, and millions of blue collar workers turned the volume up on their sets and phones, as the president addressed the nation.

"Good morning, my fellow Americans. Last night, an evil, and despicable act of war was enacted upon the United States. Thousands of lives were suddenly ended in a horrible act of treason against the Treaty on the Prohibition of Nuclear Weapons. A nuclear attack was successfully launched on American soil and a great many people have been moved to defend our nation. These acts have shocked us, but they will not shake us. They have taken our families and loved ones, but not without consequence. I have implemented our nation's response plan and have enacted our military to take every precaution against further attacks. The source of these attacks has been eliminated, but this is not the end of conflict. We are at war. My first priority, beyond defensive measures, is to ensure the safety of our survivors. The military has been deployed to the affected areas of our nation. Perimeters have been set around the detonation point and refugee camps established to treat those affected by the attack. We are doing everything we can to bring help to those that need it. Our first priority is to help all who are injured and take every precaution to protect our nation from further attacks. Trust, my fellow Americans, is our key now to assess our damages, aid our people, and bring swift justice to those behind these evil acts. I've directed every resource to this prerogative. We stand together, as one Nation, under God. This morning, I ask for your prayers to all who we have lost, to all who grieve, for all whose lives have been shattered and I pray for comfort that comes from the highest power of all, just as we read in Psalm 23: *"Yea, though I walk through the valley of the shadow of death, I will fear no evil: for thou art with me"*. This is a day that will stand in the annals of American history. Let us stand together as one, and make it one that is remembered for the harboring of peace and restoration, in a time of treason and distrust. Let us stand together as one, my fellow Americans. One nation, under God, indivisible, with liberty and justice for all. Thank you and God bless, America."

50

The road ran smooth under the Expedition's wheels and Curt eased the brake as he came upon the stop sign at the intersection of N Colbert and E Pecan St. He clicked on his blinker and took a right. Curt looked to his right and smiled in admiration of his beautiful wife and their baby boy. After stopping, back at the Flying J, it had taken a few hours to get him to go back down again, but now everyone in the car was silent. Light snores issued from the backseat and Curt's eyes bobbed up to his rearview. Each of them slept, their heads in the slings of their seatbelts. A line of drool sept from Bobby's mouth onto the shoulder of his hoodie. He was glad Adrian slept, too. Lord knew she needed it and that Bobby got enough. The boy slept more of the time than he was awake, seemingly, but he was a growing boy, and he was sure Adrian slept her fair share, too. He was just biased because she was his baby girl. Curt grinned and looked back toward the road.

The clock on the dash read 9:58 p.m. That meant 10:58 p.m. His mouth opened in a yawn and he stifled the noise. In the cupholder an empty chug jug cup of coffee sat totally wasted, as Bobby would put it. He'd done the damage about four hours before, but it had done him good. After their stop for refueling, and waiting on the kids and Marie to go to the bathroom, and checking tiny Tim's diaper, they hit the road again and were back out of Missouri and into Oklahoma in no time. They'd made the entire second half of the trip back home from Trenton in less than five hours and while driving, Curt watched the estimated time of arrival on his phone go down with slight pride.

Siri whispered from the dash that he'd take a left turn in another seven hundred feet, then arrive at his destination and he reached out and shut the directions off.

I know where I am, he thought and cruised the car down the street.

Curt let his foot off the gas and coasted, before caressing the brakes and slowing the car to a stop as they arrived home. He turned into their drive, put the gear into park, and Marie opened her eyes.

"Home?" she looked at him and smiled.

"Home," he whispered and smiled back. Tiny Tim nestled his head further into Marie's chest. Curt got out of the car and let his wife out, opening the front door for her and letting her in and the two managed to get Tim into bed without waking him up. As he started back outside again, Marie grabbed his wrist.

"Do you want any help with the suitcases?"

Curt nodded that he didn't, kissed his wife, and sent her off to bed. He stepped back outside and took the keys from the ignition. The interior light came on and Adrian and Bobby blinked awake, before stumbling inside. As he unloaded their luggage from the cargo, a smile stayed on his lips, as did the warmth from his wife's kiss. He lugged the bags from the back of the Ford and carried them inside, one by one, then locked the vehicle. His mind went to his wife, and crawling into bed with her, as he grappled with the suitcases, and lying beside her naked and sleeping together. Doctor's orders. *Yes sir,* he thought and smiled.

Curt locked the front door behind him and left their luggage in the foyer to unpack tomorrow. His hand flicked off the porchlights as he crossed into the hallway. Outside, the engine of the Ford clicked, cooling off in the dark. A warm summer wind blew down the street, rustling the bright green trees of the suburban homes. The neighborhood lay asleep and nothing moved. Bicycles and footballs rested in trimmed lawns. Several windows lit up with late night television. Most sat dark. Almost nothing sounded except the breeze. Far off traffic hummed in the air and the Expedition's engine ticked like a clock. In the near silence, from the undercarriage of the Ford, a single pregnant roach slipped onto the ground and into the sewer.

September 15th, 2024 - January 27th, 2025

I love you, Makenna

-BK

About the Author

Blake Kourik lives in Springfield, Missouri. So far, he's had no problems with bugs.

Printed in Dunstable, United Kingdom